T0345801

Over the
Bridge

Over the Bridge

Mohamed El-Bisatie

Translated by Nancy Roberts

The American University in Cairo Press
Cairo   New York

First published in 2006 by
The American University in Cairo Press
113 Sharia Kasr el Aini, Cairo, Egypt
420 Fifth Avenue, New York, NY 10018
www.aucpress.com

Dar al Kutub No. 14097/05
ISBN 977 424 974 7

Designed by Fatiha Bouzidi/AUC Press Design Center
Printed in Egypt

And there was evening, and there was morning. . . .

One

When had the idea come to him?

It may have occurred to him some time back, but without his paying any attention to it. It would flash through his mind, then disappear. Then in a moment, it materialized. He'd been looking askance at it, not wanting to give it any serious thought just yet. He'd preferred to keep it at a distance for a while.

He took leave of his rooftop quarters at the same time he did every day—7:00 a.m. Before descending the stairs, he cast a glance around the spacious roof. Some of the neighbors might throw litter in the corners when he wasn't looking. However, thanks to his uncompromising fastidiousness, the roof proper remained clean and bare. On moonlit nights he liked to walk around on the roof. Every now and then he would lean up against the roof wall, looking out from his elevated perch at the far-flung lights, and at the people and the cars, which, viewed from above, appeared as tiny as so many children's toys.

He donned an ancient overcoat with a threadbare collar and sleeves that were fraying at the ends. He wore it winter and summer. In the beginning, he'd worn it in order to cover up his dirty clothes, which he frequently forgot to wash. Then he'd gotten used to the thing.

He came down the stairs with a dignified gait. It was a five-story building, with two flats on each floor. The flats were small, consisting of nothing but a bedroom and a living room. However, he'd never gone into any of them. His relations with the neighbors were limited to passing greetings. Neither he nor they had any desire for more than that. On occasion he would encounter one of the neighbor ladies: a middle-aged women whose husband, he'd heard, worked on the rotation system, and who would sometimes be gone away on duty for days at a time. Bent over sweeping her front doorstep, she would look at him with no attempt to conceal the desire in her eyes. Her ample bosom would peek out from the neck opening in her blouse, the uppermost button of which she'd left undone. He would avoid her glance. For her, he represented a 'safe' relationship. Single. In the same building. Just a few steps away. Besides, no one would wonder why she'd gone up to the roof. When her laundry rack was full, she would hang the rest of her clothes out on the roof. Besides, she might need to come up in order to adjust the television antenna, or for any of a number of reasons.

But pretty or not, he didn't want her. Nor did he want anyone else, for that matter. She'd only bring trouble. He couldn't imagine himself with a woman in the room, and in fact, he didn't want anybody in his place of retreat. As things were, he could relax in bed and let his mind wander here and there. He preferred to imagine them moving about in the room in just the way he desired, and whispering just the words he wanted to hear. His neighbor had made one attempt, which had been the first and the last. Even so, there was still an invitation in her eyes. She had come up to the roof one day, and he had caught a glimpse of her through the door to his room, which was ajar. She was wearing a housedress and plush slippers on her feet. She walked over to the television antenna, then came back and stood in his doorway, leaning her shoulder against the doorjamb. Standing with her feet close together, her fingers moved lightly over her bosom. His things were scattered haphazardly all over the room and he was lying in bed.

With her eyes fixed on his, she asked him to help her adjust the direction of the antenna, explaining that the picture wasn't clear in her flat and that the soap opera was about to start.

He said he didn't know anything about antennas and that she could figure out which way to turn it by looking at some other antenna in the vicinity.

As though she hadn't heard him, she went on standing right where she was, looking around this way and that.

She asked him where he put his television.

He said he didn't have one.

"Don't you watch the soap opera?" she asked.

He made no reply.

"I was thinking I might watch it at his place," she muttered to herself.

Glancing over at him one final time, she turned and walked away, her steps still audible on the roof. However, there was no need for him to shut the door, since he knew she wouldn't be coming back.

The narrow side street led to the bus stop, where he caught a bus to the Department of Security where he worked as an auditor. He had fifteen minutes left to finish his breakfast.

A number of employees and laborers were gathered around the fuul vendor's cart behind the building. The employees carried their plates and pita bread to a wooden table and stood around it as they ate, while the laborers stayed at the cart. He eyed his own plate, savoring the aroma and the hot steam, and the idea came to him again. As the moments passed, he stole a glance at the faces before him as the steam wafted gently upward from their plates. Many an idea had come to him, then gone. However, this one in particular kept coming back with such insistence that once, as he was leaving the fuul cart, he said to himself, "It's so simple. Like all great ideas!"

His office was in the corner of a large room shared by ten employees. He was lost in thought, pondering his idea. All he needed was to get some papers ready, and that would be that. He had enough experience by now to prepare them with the utmost precision. The first step was the one he always hesitated to take. But once that was done, nothing would be able to stop him.

So, why not get started?

In an envelope he placed some blank sheets of paper bearing the department letterhead and the eagle stamp. He had an old one that they'd wanted to make obsolete a long time ago when a new stamp had arrived, and he'd managed to hide it away. At the time, he hadn't known why he wanted to have one. Perhaps because of the power it represented. He came across it among a bunch of odds and ends in the bottom of the drawer and, together with the inkpad, stuffed it into the envelope. He would take it with him when he went home, where he could plan out his venture in peace and quiet.

Sitting at his desk lethargically, he told himself he wouldn't think about the matter until he'd gotten back to his room. He could produce a good forgery of the signatures of all the officials whose signatures he'd be needing, including that of the minister. Just for fun, he'd trained his hand at it during his spare time at the office. Whenever a new official would come and he would see his signature on some papers before him, he would try to imitate it. He would place a transparency on top of the signature, then trace it several times. There was only one person whose signature he hadn't tried to mimic—the head of the personnel department. The man had an aversion to him, a fact he announced through gestures of the hand and the expressions on his face. As soon as he came into his office, the head of the personnel department would take off his jacket and hang it on a nearby clothes rack, keeping on an open vest that revealed his snow-white shirt and the necktie that he changed every day. On the occasions when he would come into the man's office for him to sign some papers, the latter would gesture to him with his hand to leave them on the desk and leave. He didn't even bother to look up at him. Instead, he contented himself with a wave of the hand, the purple gemstone in the ring he wore on his little finger sparkling in the light.

Once when he ran into him in the corridor, he stopped him. Then, examining his overcoat from top to bottom with a look of disgust on his face, he asked, "Where did you buy that?"

"I don't remember. It was some time ago."

"Yes, a long time."

Then he walked away.

He'd never been excited about the idea of imitating his signature. He didn't reciprocate the man's dislike of him. He had simply never felt excited about the idea. He had seen his signature on numerous papers, but it had never caught his attention. It was ordinary. Like thousands of other signatures he'd seen, and which had never inspired a desire in him to imitate them. But now he would need it for his project. He pulled a copy of an administrative decree bearing the man's signature out of a file in front of him and stuck it into the envelope he was planning to take home with him. Ten minutes, and he'd have it down pat. The next day was Friday, and he could devote himself to getting the necessary papers ready to take their course on Saturday.

On his way out, he passed by some used furniture stores in the 'Ataba district and bought a desk, a chair, and a typewriter. He'd be needing the typewriter, so if he'd had to, he would even have bought a new one. The auditing section was the last stop for all monetary activity in the department. This was the section that delivered the final word, after which a check for payments due would be made out. The enclosures that had suffered for so long and which had been circulated among countless offices until the check had been drafted, as well as memoranda, decrees, and so on, would all be placed in a file that would make its way to the filing section, where they would rot. And who would ask about them after that? If a problem ever arose, they would invariably refer the inquiry back to the auditor concerned, in which event he would be available to answer their questions, or even to pretend to go down to the filing section to check on the nonexistent file. The Khaldiya Police Station: that's what it would be called. Khaldiya: a small town with a tribal stamp. The names of towns there were so numerous, nobody could remember them all. Besides, it bore a close resemblance to the names in general circulation. Who would ever stop to think that it was an imaginary police station? Or that the town itself was nonexistent? He would get the enclosures ready the next day: the personnel affairs memorandum, the minister's decree, and the police station's payroll. He might be able to get away with not writing the personnel affairs' memorandum, since the personnel department generally preferred to keep its memoranda in its own files, and would content itself with the relevant employee's signature on the disbursement form. This being the case, he wouldn't be obliged to imitate the department head's signature after all, and he could simply supply the minister's decree which read: "Based on the relevant statutes, for the sake of effective work, and in keeping with the authority vested in us, we have hereby seen fit to establish a police station in the city of Khaldiya."

Two

It was Friday evening and he had finished preparing the needed paperwork. He stood leaning against the rooftop wall and looking out at the horizon, which was tinted with the reddish glow of twilight. He tried to picture this city of his that had just come into existence. It would be on both banks of the Nile. Khaldiya. A nice name. And the police station would be white. Two stories. An old villa that had been remodeled and rented out, its rent to be paid once a year. How much would the rent be? He'd think about that later. The payroll was still spread out on the desk in his room. It still needed one little thing that hadn't occurred to him when he'd been planning things out, namely, a disbursement officer. The payroll check would be issued in his name, and he would cash it himself at the bank, since it isn't allowed to endorse a payroll check or other checks of its type. It's the disbursement officer who is supposed to deliver the salaries to the employees, at which point they sign the payroll to indicate their receipt of the amount due them. The officer, of course, is also an employee at the police station and his name is also on the payroll. Who should it be? He ruled out his colleagues at the Security Department. No, it would have to be someone who was ignorant of financial matters and who would believe whatever story he happened to tell him. Who? He remembered someone he'd met at the coffee shop. Younis. He had the name of one of the prophets, but none of their virtues. He smiled and headed back to his room.

Sometimes he would go to a coffee shop on a quiet side street. He'd take a corner seat, smoke the water pipe and drink tea, watch the customers as they made their usual ruckus, then quickly get bored and leave.

One day someone came and sat beside him. Or rather, not exactly beside him, since there was an empty seat between them. Then on a later occasion, he sat right next to him. In fact, he rested his elbow on the small table where they were sitting. His glass of tea was still full, and he watched it out of the corner of his eye as it wobbled.

The man said his name was Younis.

He pretended not to have heard him, and as soon as he finished his tea, he got up and left.

On subsequent visits to the coffee shop, Younis continued coming to his table. Then one day he starting telling him about the difficult circumstances he was going through. A petty employee in the archives section of the Ministry of Housing, his salary wasn't enough to cover even two meals a day of bread and fuul mudammas for him and his family. What terrified him was the thought that one of his three children might fall ill, in which event he didn't know what he would do. His wife had begun working, cleaning houses three times a week. She was someone who had lived all her life at home, cared for and respected, and his salary had been enough for them. They'd been able to afford fruit and new clothes. But now, they had to buy them used from carts in the street, and sometimes his wife would bring some home from the houses where she was employed.

He fell silent for a while and turned his face away. And leftover food, too.

Who would have believed that a day would come when he would be waiting for leftovers from other people's houses? And when she came home empty-handed, it was a miserable day for everybody. He didn't understand what was happening, but things had changed. What his wife was making was helping to pay for the children's needs, including school fees and books.

He fell silent again, his head lowered.

What pained him was for his wife to have to go out to work in other people's houses. She would dress like a cleaning lady: she'd put on a jilbab with a pair of his old pajama trousers underneath, plastic slippers, and a scarf around her head. Of course she wouldn't go wearing a dress and shoes. That would be ridiculous.

Besides which, she had started talking like other cleaning ladies. Even her hand gestures were starting to resemble theirs.

Still hanging his head, he said he was looking for an afternoon job. Maybe things would get better.

"What kind of work do you do?" Younis asked.

He didn't give out information about himself to anyone.

"I work at the Governorate," he said.

"The Governorate?"

Gazing at him with his languid eyes, Younis asked, "What do you do there?"

"Whatever . . ."

Content with his response, Younis thrust his hands between his knees and hunched forward.

A little while later he asked him if he could find him a job there. The Governorate stays open late. He happened to have passed by it at night and had seen its windows lit up, with shadows moving behind the glass panes. He could work four or five hours. He could do anything, even if it meant making tea and coffee for people, in a canteen, for example.

Sometimes Younis would escort him back from the coffee shop. On their way he would point to a side street entrance saying, "That's where I live. The fourth house on the right, ground floor."

Then he would insist on walking him all the way to the building where he lived. This didn't go over very well with him, as he wasn't anxious to have Younis knocking on the door to his room some day, so he would take leave of him abruptly.

Younis was the right person, though he didn't know his full name. He'd be turning the papers in to his boss the next day along with the payrolls for other police departments, so he wouldn't be able to wait several days until he met up with this Younis at the coffee shop again. However, he did know the street where he lived, and maybe the house as well, and he could ask about him. If he didn't agree, he'd look for somebody else. He was sure to agree, though.

He put on his overcoat and headed down the stairs.

Younis came out when he called him. He stood in the doorway, looking at him in astonishment. Barefoot, he was wearing flannel, short-sleeved pajamas. He followed him inside the house. In the center of the cramped living room there were the remains of a mat, four armchairs with small wooden slats across each seat, and whose innards hung down to the floor. Younis brought a cushion from somewhere and placed it on one of the seats. Once he'd sat down, he caught sight of Younis's three children as they stood looking at him from a bedroom doorway. Among them was a twelve-year-old girl. Their clothes were clean and they had thongs on their feet. He takes care of his children, he thought. An encouraging sign.

Younis apologized, explaining that his wife was still at work, but would be back any minute. A fleeting glance at his children, and they disappeared inside the bedroom and closed the door.

He took pleasure in coming and in what he would say and observe. He had conjured it all up in his imagination on the way to Younis's house.

He said, "You asked me some time ago to help you look for a job."

"Yes!" Younis replied in a near shout.

"You're a ministry employee, so it wouldn't be fitting for you to work as an office boy who makes coffee and tea."

Younis shrank into his seat again, his hands between his knees.

"However, an opportunity has opened up, a temporary one that might become permanent."

He paused briefly, then continued, "You'd work as a disbursement officer. The monthly salary is five hundred pounds."

Younis didn't budge. Listening intently, he seemed to be waiting for him to say something else.

"Do you accept?"

"What is it that I'm supposed to accept?"

"The job, as disbursement officer."

"Disbursement officer? Me?"

His voice grew louder, with a slight tone of protest as though he hadn't decided yet whether someone was playing games with him.

He explained the situation to him further, saying, "The work is associated with the Governorate, but it's overseen by a foreign establishment. The employees' salaries are high. The Governorate prepares the payroll for the Egyptian workforce. However, the disbursement officer has unexpectedly fallen ill. He's in the hospital now for surgery, and his condition isn't encouraging. It's anybody's guess what will happen with him. However, the work is ongoing."

The whole story was a fabrication, but as he told it, it sounded convincing.

As he spoke, Younis crept to the edge of his seat, his body rigid.

"A disbursement officer with a salary of five hundred pounds," he murmured, "for somebody with average qualifications, like me. After fifteen years of service, all I make is one hundred twenty pounds."

"Yes, but foreign companies . . ."

"And I'll get the same salary, five hundred pounds?"

"Yes, in addition to rewards that are issued from time to time."

"Rewards?"

"Every disbursement statement, not including those for purchases and repairs, will include your name in your capacity as disbursement officer."

"And when the original disbursement officer recovers?"

"At that time, if they're happy with your performance, they may give you some other position."

"And my work at the Ministry of Housing?"

"This is what led me to come discuss the matter with you. After all, you wouldn't want to sacrifice your long years of service and your retirement pay, especially given the fact that there are no retirement benefits associated with the position of disbursement officer. Your new job will take all of ten minutes. You accompany me to the bank, you cash the check, you receive your reimbursement and sign the statement to indicate receipt of the amount due you. Then I take the cash and deliver it, together with the statement, to the work site official who will come to my office for this purpose. Consequently, we need to keep quiet about this. After all, as you know, you're not permitted to accept employment outside of your job at the ministry. A check will need to be cashed in the next few days, if you're interested."

"But why don't you take the job for yourself?" asked Younis. "It's five hundred pounds that you're in need of."

As he spoke, he was looking at his overcoat's threadbare collar.

"How would you know? I've had another job for some time now. Don't look at my clothes. I have plenty, but I haven't changed my lifestyle so as not to attract attention. Meanwhile, I've held onto my original job."

"And where is your original job?"

"In one of the ministries."

"You told me you worked at the Governorate."

"That's what I told you."

Eventually Younis agreed. He gave him his full name and three samples of his signature for him to deliver to the bank. Then he left.

The papers he needed were now complete. The police chief held the rank of lieutenant colonel, and the investigations assistant held the rank of major. There was also a colonel, first and second lieutenants, an investigations officer with a rank of first lieutenant, a special technical sergeant, as well as first-class, second-class and third-class technical sergeants. Four sergeants, seven corporals, and twenty soldiers from Central Security, as well as six civil clerks including the disbursement officer, brought the total payroll to 25,234 Egyptian pounds.

He stood for a moment looking at the statement on the desk. The employees had now come into existence, as had the city. He went out on to the roof for a stroll.

The cashing of the check took only fifteen minutes. Younis was waiting for him in front of the bank wearing a reasonable-looking jacket. He stood beside him in front of the teller's window in his capacity as his escort. Then he took the small briefcase from him and gave him the five hundred pounds. Younis stared at him questioningly the entire time.

He flagged a taxi and went with Younis to deliver him to his ministry. Then he went to another bank where he opened an account in his own name and deposited the money.

Nothing in his life changed, except for a bag of fruit that he would bring home from time to time on his way back from work. He would put it in a corner of the room, and sometimes forget it, only to be reminded of it by the smell it gave off when it started to rot, whereupon he would throw it into the empty lot behind the building.

His bank account swelled steadily from one month to the next, and he ended up opening accounts in four other banks as well, so as to avoid drawing attention to himself.

Apart from the times when he went to the coffee shop, he spent his evenings lying in bed or leaning against the rooftop wall, where the high elevation allowed him to see long distances.

He only broke out of his lethargy when it was time to draft the payroll. Before sitting down to his desk, he tried to picture the city and its inhabitants, the police station and the activity of the people who worked there. However, his imagination wasn't coming through for him. All he managed to conjure up was an image of the white building where the station was located. There was no movement either in front of it or inside of it. He was in the position to make decisions to issue rewards and financial incentives in order to spur activity at the station. But how was he to do that when he couldn't conjure up an image of the place?

He put on his overcoat over his pajamas and went out.

He had spied a furniture repair shop nearby. Where was the place? He finally came to it. He bought a slab of thin plywood, two meters long and one meter wide, with a frame around it.

"Could you give it a non-glossy gray tone?" he asked.

"What do you need it for?"

"A picture, possibly."

Once the color had dried, he took it and left. On his way back, he bought a large amount of modeling clay of various colors.

He placed the board on the desk. A model of the city of Khaldiya was what he needed. He had the time, and the modeling clay, and he wouldn't come out of his room until he saw it before him with its people, its hustle and bustle, and the police station as well.

A glass of tea. No harm in that. Humming a tune, he sashayed to the kitchen to get the tea ready.

And now: First the river. A narrow, slightly winding strip of brown modeling clay that divides the town, like all towns in Upper Egypt, into two halves. The new quarter is characterized by its modern architecture, its broad, straight streets, streetlights only a short distance apart that turn the night into day, two- and one-story villas surrounded by low trees—mostly lemon and with occasional rosebushes and jasmine vines, for example, whose fragrance wafts throughout the neighborhood. There are mansions with broad marble staircases and colored gravel walkways, and wide verandas where it's nice to have one's breakfast. Standing on the veranda one might see the lady of the house, generally of middle age and who, when she starts getting older, will most likely move to a flat in the capital. From time to time you'll see her wearing a top with thin shoulder straps, or she might be still in a nightgown that reveals her pretty shoulders. She calls out in a singsong voice that carries outside the walls, and is answered by a servant who's watching over the woman's young daughter on the garden swing. They exchange words. So much for the people.

There are four pontoons in the river. No harm in that. Four is enough for entertainment on the side that isn't supposed to come to the knowledge of the ladies who occupy the mansions and villas: Card playing. Hot breaths. Perhaps young girls. A special taste that's catered to in secret. But not all of them. I have to be fair, neutral. There are also folks with other predilections and who pursue their activity in the open. And there are still others with no predilections at all, for whom there is just family life without problems, peace and quiet. What's the harm in young girls, booze, and drugs? The folks there have laid down the laws that suit them, that forbid some things and allow others. We'll see. Despite my neutrality, I might be a bit biased. The new quarter on the other side of the river is inhabited by businessmen and big-time merchants, and people in positions of authority. Some flats for the red light district. There isn't a town without one. Two flats. No, we'll make it three. And who uses them? Whoever wants to, has the private space, and the ability to spend. And perhaps other types, too. The regular flats' residents, for example. There are those among them who want to do it, if only just once in their lives, and even if it means stealing some of their wives' jewelry. And visitors. And transients. There's nothing wrong with their being there. The three flats are owned by a woman. What's she like? We'll get to that later. It creates an exciting atmosphere, hot situations. After all, how can life be tolerable without some friction?

The police station is here—for the first time he was discovering what agile fingers he had as they pressed the pieces of clay, softening and shaping them with lightning speed—in the new quarter, whose residents are always being targeted by someone. Located not far from the riverbank and facing the old quarter on the other side, it's in an old two-story villa painted a non-glossy white with a sign on the front that reads, "Khaldiya Police Station." Three motorboats at anchor are guarded by a soldier. There's no harm in there being river patrols. An appendix to the payroll includes motorboat drivers, a recent addition based on security requirements. There are six police cars to assist in carrying out assignments, including one that's set aside exclusively for the police inspector and a half-size pickup truck parked in the garage behind the station. The garage is roofed with wood and palm leaves. Oh! We forgot the casinos. Two of them: one on the riverbank and another not far from it on the same bank. There are large supermarkets for people to roam around in, pushing small shopping carts in front of them. There are other commercial establishments, too: clothing stores, furniture stores, hair salons, flower shops, all sorts. After all, they're the main thing that distinguishes the new quarter, with clientele drawn from neighboring towns.

And now we cross the river to the other bank. But first, a cup of tea.

It was past midnight. He'd never stayed up this late before. A pain shot through his back from the way he'd been hunched over the desk. As he stood looking at the model, he felt pleased. He had enough modeling clay for the other bank. And if he had some left after that, he could add another neighborhood or two. They'd be interesting, these neighborhoods: set apart, with their own special flavor.

He walked unhurriedly around the roof. There were lights as far as the eye could see, many of which had now gone out, while the loud noises had died down. Everyone to his place of refuge. Speaking of which, he thought: The notion of a place of refuge evolved over the years from sleeping in the open to cave dwelling, then to life in huts, and so on until it reached the level of high-rise apartment buildings. We want to be safe while we're asleep, not to be taken unawares. Indeed, even in modern high rises we've taken to installing alarm systems, automatic doors, and bars on the windows.

He came back to his seat.

Where were we? In the old quarter, the town's birthplace: covered with the dust of long years past and with wounds, scars, and bruises too numerous to count. He saw a lot. There was a bridge that connected the two banks. It was a broad, well-lit bridge that could also be raised. The argument behind this was that it allowed sailboats to pass through. Or so it was said. However, although raising the bridge would indeed allow any sailboat to pass through, the true purpose behind it was to deal with times of disturbance—in other words, to isolate each of the banks from the other.

And thus you see, Mr. Inspector, that I've prepared the place for you in a way that will make it easier for you to do your job. The choice is yours. Given its wealth and opulence, the new quarter is also somebody's target. As for the old quarter, it's so congested, so filled with hotbeds of rage it could go up in flames with the greatest of ease.

Ah, and we won't forget the old ferryboat, the way people used to get across the river before the bridge was built. Anchored not far from the bridge, it's lost its splendor and turned a clay color. Leaning up against the bank, huge rats nest there now, while the ramshackle houses along that side of the river are so close together, they nearly pass into each other. Their roofs are in total disrepair, yet they're still intact despite the passing of the years and the tribulations they've seen. There are some blind alleys, and others that lead to houses whose doors are wide open and which lead, in turn, to an alley on the other side, like a kind of corridor. The daily lives of the folks on both sides consist of cooking, laundry, clamor, and the like. They pay no attention to passersby and passersby pay no attention to them. One of these days you'll enter the area with your police patrol, the regular patrol, and it will be by night. You'll find them sleeping on both sides, while folks on each side spread out two blankets on a taut rope to give them some privacy during their slumber. And there's a kerosene lamp hanging in a small window that lights the way for those passing through.

You nearly retreat, fearing that it might be an ambush. However, the men with you have already come in from behind, and turning back would cause a commotion that you wouldn't want. You're reassured when you see the other alley facing you through the open door, lit up by the stars. It's entirely empty, with cats frolicking happily here and there, and the doors and windows of the houses are closed. You see feet, legs and arms protruding from beneath the edge of the taut blankets, and you take care not to allow your horse to step on them. Abundant shops, some of them little more than holes in the wall, coffee shops that stay open till morning, and kiosks with seats arranged outside them as an alternative to the coffee shops and restaurants. Schools, including a secondary school for religious sciences and a girls' secondary school. A shrine devoted to a venerable sheikh that people used to visit in order to receive his blessing, now abandoned. A railroad station and a track that were deserted after they transferred the station to the new quarter. The old station is still standing, though, with the promise that they'll open another railroad line to it. In the background are vast agricultural lands, their hue a brilliant green, with animal enclosures, an irrigation canal and ditches that branch off from it, and two factories, one for textiles and another for cement. The dust from the latter hovers over the houses, and most of the area's residents are afflicted with lung disease. No matter, though. Life is bound to have its troubles.

Now the model was finished.

As he stood wiping his hands with a small towel, the light of dawn flooded the roof, the sun's rays stealing into the room through the open door.

Khaldiya. A sign bearing the town's name. Where should it be? On the building that used to house the old station. If I see one morning there, I can rest. The sun rises. The old quarter is bustling with noisy activity. The alleyways and streets are filled with people, most of whom will filter out to the fields, the two factories and the schools. Laden minibuses move away from their stops. Some of them head for the bridge on their way to the new quarter, which is still in a state of repose, most of their passengers being girls and women who work in houses there.

Now I can see it, and the police station, too.

Three

He went out.

He hadn't been to the coffee shop for two weeks, so he said to himself: I'll take a walk and see people.

He had a small ebony cane that he'd bought from a street vendor a long time before, then forgotten. He happened to spy it under the bed, so he slipped it under his arm.

He took a seat in his corner of the coffee shop. Not long afterward Younis came in, happy with himself and the world.

"You finally came!" he shouted jubilantly. "I'd been wondering where you went."

Younis took his right hand in both of his hands and shook it warmly, then sat down on the seat next to him. He was wearing a new blue suit, a brightly colored necktie, and a pink shirt, with a handkerchief of the same color that peeked out of his upper pocket.

He took out a pack of Marlboro cigarettes and a lighter and placed them on the table.

"I've never seen you smoke before."

"I decided I'd try it. I'd been away from it for a long time. If I knew where you lived, I would have come to see you."

"What's your news?"

"I'm doing just great."

When the waiter brought the orders, he murmured jokingly to Younis as usual, "Who gave to you so that you could give to us, Uncle Younis?"

Younis smiled at him affectionately.

"What did people at work say when they saw your new clothes?"

"Nothing. I told them I'd joined a cooperative and was the first to collect my share. The drinks will be on me this time."

He nodded wordlessly and took a long drag on the water pipe. Younis leaned forward and with his fingernail, steadied a hot coal that was about to fall off the bowl saying, "We've rented a new flat."

He remained silent and avoided looking at him.

"I'd wanted to tell you about it before, since you might have another opinion. I came to the coffee shop every night, but didn't find you."

He maintained his silence, eyeing the live coals on the water pipe bowl as they alternately glowed and died down.

"I thought to myself: Let's give ourselves a little more room. The girl's started to grow up and needs a bedroom of her own, and the two boys can stay in another one. We've come up in the world, from the ground floor to the third floor, and from the alleyway to the main street. And we're paying for it in installments. If only you'd seen the girl! She was jumping for joy. She has a white wardrobe with a double-leaf door, a white bed, and a little dressing table of the same color. She keeps her clothes neat and hangs pictures on the walls: pictures of actors and actresses. Her mother says to her, 'Can't you find anything else to hang on your walls?' We've got a color TV, too. We had a black-and-white, but we got tired of fixing it and gave it to the doorman."

"And your wife?"

"I told her I got a raise, and that they'd added allowances and a cost-of-living bonus. She's stopped working. She wanted to continue. She said, 'It adds to the blessing.' But I wouldn't let her. I said to her, 'God's provided enough and more for us. You belong at home.' It's incredible. She's shrunk to half her previous size, she's gotten varicose veins in her legs, and her face has lost its color. She isn't what she used to be."

"Did you leave the old flat?"

"No. We pay an old rent, just two pounds a month. You know. Just in case we need it, I thought, with all its furniture and everything else in it. Who knows? There might be times when I want to have some time to myself and think at my leisure, to contemplate the state of the world. There's no end to the racket the kids make, with the television and the tape player both on full blast. And after you've given them something, you don't want to scold them for it."

He fell silent. Then suddenly he laughed and blushed slightly.

"I'll be frank with you. There's a woman. You're my friend and have been so good to me. Why should I keep it from you? Yeah, a woman. She lives in the old apartment building. Divorced. She used to come on to me and I'd pretend not to notice. Her husband left her the flat in return for her leaving the boy with him. She and my wife don't like each other. My wife used to say that this woman's husband hadn't divorced her for no reason, especially after the stories he used to hear about her. And after she got to know my wife, she said, 'She's all dried up and skinny. What do you see in her? There isn't a man on earth who'd want to sleep with her. Her bones would hurt him the entire time.' Really, that's what she says! And other things, too. But she's fun to be with. The first time she saw me coming into the old flat after we'd evacuated it, she had her back to me. Then she turned around and said, 'All right, then. Instead of your eyes crawling down my back, come on up.' 'No,' I said to her, 'you come down.' She shrugged her shoulders and went up to her flat. A day or so later, though, she came down. She really did."

He looked at him without saying more, then continued, "Are you bothered by what I'm saying? You know!" he added, laughing and shaking his head slightly.

"Not at all. It's an interesting story. Go on."

"Well, I was on my way to the old flat with a bag of plums in my hand, and no sooner had I opened the door than I found her looking over my shoulder. She said, 'And you've left everything here. The bed, the wardrobe, the dining table, and the stove. It's just as well, though. The stuff's no good any more. It wouldn't hold up if you tried to take it apart, move it and put it back together again. Your wife is such a donkey, she doesn't know how to take care of anything. Not even her clothes. She might have a new gallabiya, and before you know it, it looks miserable on her.'"

He chuckled, shaking his head and feet.

"She badmouths my wife, and I laugh. What can I say to her? The things she says are funny."

He fell silent, then murmured, "They really are . . ."

More silence, then after a moment he resumed his story.

"The bag caught her eye and she asked, 'What's in there?' She leaned in closer to peek inside. 'Plums? You're planning on eating some, then. I'll wash them for you.' She was wearing a jilbab and slippers on her feet. She lifted the bottom of her jilbab as she stood at the sink. And what a leg. Plump and healthy-looking. She put the plums on a plate and walked into the bedroom with me behind her. Yep. It was a happy day."

He turned to look at the other customers in the coffee shop, but it was as though he didn't see anyone.

He said, "You haven't even told me your name."

"What do you need it for? Go ahead with your story."

"What shall I call you?"

"Call me Salem."

"Is that your name?"

"Call me that and I'll answer to it."

"And when I need you, how shall I contact you?"

"I'll contact you. In another couple of days we'll cash a check."

"The first of the month is still a long way off."

"The first of the month is for salaries. This is a check for rewards."

"I see. And do I have a share in it?"

"Of course. You have a share of every check. The disbursement officer's name is always on the statement. But your share in this one is less than your salary—three hundred pounds."

"Wonderful."

"Let's go."

The two of them left.

The street had become less busy as the night wore on. As they walked side by side down the sidewalk, Younis caught sight of the cane.

"I've never seen that with you before."

"I've had it for some time."

"It's pretty. I want one. Where did you get it?"

"From a vendor on the street. Do you pay her?"

"Who?"

"Your neighbor."

"I never have. I might take a half-kilo of shish kebab with me, or fruit. Once I took her a ring, and another time I took her some earrings. Women like presents. But if you don't like it . . ."

"Do as you wish."

"She wants to marry me. She's said so directly. She wants to dupe her ex-husband. Women!"

"And you?"

"I play along with her. She's got a beautiful body. You seem busy."

"Yeah, I've got to get home."

"You see? I'm starting to understand you."

And they parted.

Four

He ate his dinner standing up, looking at the model.

And now, Mr. Inspector, you're going to do some work. You have a car. However, I'd like to see you on horseback. The horse is black. According to your rules, the inspector doesn't go out on patrol. The lieutenant does that. You'll issue orders for there to be two patrols, one of which will be under your command. I'm not inclined to make you kind or compassionate. Not even your appearance will give that impression: pointed features, a beak-like nose, and shoulders that are hunched as though you were getting ready to pounce. You deal with thieves and murderers, the most underhanded types. Your profession has left its stamp on you. You'll be vicious, cruel, and quick to lose your temper. There's no reason there can't be moments when you overflow with sweetness. However, those moments will be few and far between. When they come, you'll have no tolerance for them and you'll be quick to shake them off.

You live in a small flat not far from the police station. And what else?

He walked around the room a bit then paused in front of the model.

You don't surrender yourself to me easily. But you have no choice. What I want is what matters. That's right. But then again, I don't like that. You won't know, of course, what I'm thinking.

He went out onto the roof and paced back and forth several times, gazing at the darkened horizon. Then he went back to his desk.

You live in a small flat. We already said that. Your wife prefers to stay in the capital, her excuse being that her son is in a foreign school of the sort you don't find in Khaldiya. When the idea was first suggested, you welcomed it in silence. In the provincial towns, you want to have complete freedom of movement. What you don't know is that your wife has complained about you to her closest friend. In a word, she says you're impossible to live with. Whenever an order is issued for you to be transferred to some distant township, she's the happiest woman in the world. You have the habit of throwing your dirty clothes everywhere, including putrid-smelling socks. As soon as she gets wind of the stench, she holds her nose and starts making the rounds of the bedroom in search of them. And she finds them in the most unthinkable places: under the chairs, behind their cushions, etc. When that happens, she has to bend down in disgust to pick them up. Once time she came across a sock under the pillow. She tried in vain to understand what would have made you stuff it into a spot like that. In any case, she had to change the bed sheet and the pillowcases. Never once has a sweet word come out of your mouth. Instead, you're sullen. When she speaks to you, your mind is somewhere else rather than on her. And it's this habit more than anything else that alienates her from you. When you look at women on television, you lick your moustache with the tip of your tongue, and when you're having sex with her, you drool all over her neck so that she has to keep a handkerchief in her hand to dry it off from time to time, and she wonders why you don't hold the handkerchief yourself. And you've got thick hair under your arms with an odor that turns her stomach. When two women get together in private, they say things you'd never dream of. And get this: Sometimes you come home after she's gone to sleep. You've been drinking and smoking, and you wake her up and ask her to take off whatever she's wearing. She doesn't refuse, since she's afraid you'll get angry and start shouting in the middle of the night the way you've done on previous occasions. She's embarrassed to be naked in front of you, and your ravenous eyes wound her sensitivities. Once she's stripped down, you ask her to walk around the room a bit, so she does, while you stay in bed covered with a sheet. You play with yourself, and you think that the movement of your hand isn't visible. Overcome with desire, your hand starts to move faster and faster. The sheet billows up till it nearly comes off you. She catches a glimpse of you, but conceals her revulsion. Sometimes you come while she's still walking around the room, in which case she has to change the sheets that have been polluted by your secretions. Then she gets dressed and goes to sleep. Other times, you call to her before you come and she lies down beside you, her body devoid of desire. It's lost its spirit. But when you find her body surrendering to your embrace, you think it's on account of her own irresistible desire, and you exhale rapturously. She looks over your shoulder at the bedroom door that you usually forget to close. I wish your son would walk in on you, and I almost make it happen, then I think better of it. That would be a difficult situation. No matter what you have done or will do, I consider it too much for you. She's under you. You don't notice the door until she's already under you. It terrifies her to think of her son waking up from a nightmare and coming to you. That happens with him a lot. She looks out through the open door into the dimly lit living room. You whisper to her to say the kinds of things you like to hear. She clears her throat slightly, but doesn't say them. It isn't long before you come and fling yourself down, breathless. Within moments you're fast asleep and letting off a loud snore. She quietly draws herself away from you, goes to the bathroom where she rinses herself off in disgust, then goes to sleep for the rest of the night beside her son. She tells her friend that she's lost all desire to sleep with you, or with any other man for that matter. She's said all sorts of things about you, but you're clueless: You come and go with your feathers puffed up. And when she gets together with her friend, they smile at you, eyeing your face intently, and you think it's a look of admiration.

The three patrol soldiers have readied the horses and are waiting for you in front of the station. You come out of your office dressed in full uniform. You carry a leather-covered baton under your arm, your finger grasping its tip. At this time of night the station gets crowded. In the outer lobby there are some men with wounds on their heads and faces. Their clothes are spattered with blood, and they're surrounded by family members. Some people in handcuffs are standing to the side with a guard. Seeing you, a soldier rushes forward waving a bamboo stick to clear a path for you.

You mount your horse. The horses have been trained to walk with a high-stepped, showy gait, their hooves pounding the asphalt in a monotonous rhythm. You take off on your round in the new quarter. You move forward, and I move behind you. I see you but you don't see me. You sense momentarily that there's someone watching you. You turn to look behind you, then continue on your way. The new quarter is still awake. Lights are aglow on the balconies, shining through the openings in the latticework shutters over the closed windows. The pounding of the horses' hooves shatters the silence, and you see heads turning to look at you. You draw yourself up with a slight cough. The soldiers behind you are about to fall asleep from the monotonous rhythm. The trees that ring the walls of the mansions and villas unsettle you, since they provide cover for people who might seek to gain entry by stealth. However, that's what their owners want despite the fact that the walls are beautiful without them, and vary from one dwelling to the next. You know that the patrol does nothing to hinder thieves or murderers. After all, it comes and goes. However, it provides reassurance for homeowners. The eye of the law never shuts. You were once approached by some people who wanted to discuss the matter of assigning private guards to their homes and businesses.

"You're insulting me!" you shouted angrily. "Wait till I'm gone, then do whatever you like."

They responded to your tirade with smooth, tepid smiles. They know just how far they can push you and they don't want to make you angry. Never once have they held back when it came to the requisite gifts on special occasions, nor in inviting you to dinners or soirées. You're far from your family here, their guest. However, they've undertaken secretly to appoint their own private guards, one or two for every building planted among their other servants. You've seen them behind the iron gates working as gatekeepers, or bent over with their shears and scythes in small gardens within the gates, pruning the rose bushes and manicuring the lawns. You recognize them from their facial expressions and the looks in their eyes. However, you pretend not to take any notice. In fact, you've accepted it with indifference.

Robberies do take place, on an average of eighteen per year. It's a high rate. And the method is always the same. They break through the latticework that encloses the back porch using a ladder that's always in the garden. The home—a villa or mansion, and sometimes a flat—is empty, its residents out of town. You arrest the suspects from the old quarter. They're always the same faces. They spend a night or two in jail, during which time they suffer whatever they suffer. They come out later with swollen faces and bleeding heads. And throughout the time of their incarceration there's always a big crowd posted quietly outside, in front of the station and on the side streets. The people keeping vigil ask no questions and do nothing to obstruct those coming and going. Instead, they just wait. Some of them get up from where they've been sitting and cast a glance inside the station, then return to their places.

In the beginning, you were amazed that there would be women clad in black among the vigil-keepers: some of them elderly, and some of them beautiful young women with tall, svelte figures. One time, one of them caught your eye. You were coming down the outside steps and you saw her facing you. With two fingers she'd lifted the edge of her floor-length jilbab to reveal a clean, delicate foot inside an open-toed shoe. Her toenails were painted, and you glimpsed the side of a tapered leg with a stunningly glossy complexion.

You took your time coming down the stairs, your gaze fixed on her stone-rigid face. She returned your stare without even blinking. You muttered to yourself: All this beauty, and here, of all places. She may be the wife or sister of one of those good-for-nothing detainees.

They eye you wordlessly as you come and go, and late at night as you head for home, you pass through them. Some of them are lying down and fast asleep, while others are still in a squatting position and struggling to stay awake. You're consoled by the fact that they always find the private guards in the plundered houses tied up and muzzled. You search a large number of houses in the old quarter, even though you know ahead of time that you won't find anything. After all, no thief is going to keep what he's stolen at home, then sit there waiting for you. Even so, you storm the houses in the midst of screaming and wailing, leaving them in shambles. Someone whispers to you that the thieves came from another town, and you say it's a possibility. However, you're not keen on following it up, since this would mean broadening your search, and you don't have a thread of evidence to give you a lead. Besides, the purpose behind such a suggestion might be to divert attention from the old quarter and put an end to the tyranny its residents suffer. There's no end to their tricks, and you've gotten a taste of some of them yourself. You have lists of the names of all the suspects from there. Some of them are getting up in years. Even so, you bring them in. They come in sometimes on crutches, or carried on others' shoulders. No matter. And how were you to know they were in this condition?

The inquiries yield new names, and you send people out to keep an eye on them. Yet nothing turns up. Time after time you suspect that there's something amiss with the inquiries themselves. It might be pent up resentments or a settling of accounts. You've become cautious in your dealings with them. You're no longer naïve, and not so ready to be deceived by their innocent appearance.

Perhaps you remember the old story. On account of it you disappeared from the town for an entire week based on instructions from headquarters in the capital: Search for al-Umari. Ibrahim al-Umari. Wanted for interrogation. A native of the town. There were hunger strikes in the capital that lasted three days and nights. Most of the city's businesses were vandalized and their storefronts shattered. Thousands of cars were vandalized in the streets, and things reached the point where the president of the country had a helicopter stationed on the roof of his palace so that he could flee at a moment's notice. Someone had seen Ibrahim al-Umari in the midst of the crowd, shouting and egging them on. A long-time communist who'd been arrested twice before, his name was on their lists.

Given a set of reports with which you were familiar, the name wasn't new to you. You tried to recall it. In those days you were a junior officer in the federal security investigations department.

You told the investigations assistant who'd been preparing the force that was to raid al-Umari's house, "You accompany them, since you're sure you know him, and as soon as you see him, you'll remember him."

Laughing, you added jokingly, "So they won't hand over someone else to you in his place!"

You moved out at the head of the force and crossed the bridge to the old quarter, and before long the pedestrians and passersby had taken to the sides of the streets and stood in their places. And so on it went from street to street until you reached your destination.

The force attracted a large crowd, who began following them at close range, pushing and shoving. Some of them went up onto the housetops overlooking the street. The force surrounded the house and closed off the two ends of the street in front of it, as well as the street behind it. There was no outlet for escape now.

Some members of the force nearly lit into the crowds with their billy clubs to force them back. But you prevented them. There was no justification for it, you said. The panic you'd struck in their hearts by your mere coming was sufficient. And this is what's needed from time to time. It's an approach whose effectiveness you believe in, and certainly preferable to blind tyranny.

The door of the house was closed. One of the soldiers beat on it with the butt of his rifle, shouting, "Ibrahim al-Umari!"

Then silence reigned all around you. An eerie silence. Feeling a bit anxious, you cast your gaze among the faces of the people in the crowd. The soldier beat violently on the door again.

The door creaked, then slowly opened, and there emerged a tall elderly man with disheveled gray hair. He appeared to have been taking a nap, and blinked his eyes when he saw you. You looked at him pensively from atop your mount. He was too old to be the person you were after.

"Ibrahim al-Umari!" shouted the investigations assistant.

The old man looked at him, then at the others. For several moments he didn't move a muscle, then he muttered, "Who wants him?"

"He's wanted for interrogation."

He resumed his silence. Running his hand over the hair sprouting on his chin, his gaze moved unhurriedly from one face to another until it rested on yours.

"I'm his father," he said.

"And where is Ibrahim?" you asked.

His glance still fixed on your face, he asked, "Are you the new police inspector?"

"I am."

"And the other one. Where did he go?"

You marveled at the conversation taking place between the two of you and the patience you were showing this man. You made no reply.

"You all come and go," he said. "Yep . . . that's the world for you."

"Where is Ibrahim?"

"Ibrahim?"

It wasn't until later that you comprehended the expression that appeared on his face.

Pointing with his arm outstretched, he said, "Over there, near the big sycamore tree, you might find him."

He was about to turn to go back inside when the investigations assistant said to him, "Don't leave the house. If we don't find him, we're coming back to you."

Someone in the crowd shouted, "I know where it is. Come on!"

None of you paid any attention to the voice, since the tree was known to all. It was an old tree, the only sycamore in the area, and more than once had been used in police investigations as a point of reference for identifying other locations.

The force headed toward the big sycamore, with some rushing ahead of you and the rest of the crowd trailing behind. The tree was on a slight elevation some distance from the houses. Huge, with thick branches, a shepherd was sitting in its shade and grazing his seven sheep on the sparse grass. It's my favorite profession. After all, shepherds have so many distinctive qualities: indifference to worldly things, wisdom, patience, serenity, a heart-rending singing voice, and the ability to predict things, too. Sometimes their predictions come true, and when they do, people elevate them to a new rank and start to venerate them.

You halted in front of the shepherd, and the investigations assistant asked him about Ibrahim al-Umari.

The shepherd looked up. He'd been whittling a piece of bamboo with a pocketknife—apparently in the process of making an arghoul. He pointed with the piece of bamboo to an area behind him, where rows of graves stretched out into the distance.

"There," he said, "The eighth one in the third row on the left."

You looked at him uncomprehendingly, then it dawned on you. A tremor of rage swept over you, but you maintained your composure.

"Has he been there for a long time?" you asked.

"Around ten years."

You turned around with your force to make your way back to where you'd come from. The crowd of families that had been trailing you had vanished and the streets had cleared. They must have gotten the news.

You went to your office and closed the door behind you. Even after they brought in the old man and gave him a hard thrashing, you didn't calm down.

A communiqué came from headquarters in response to your own communication to them, asking you to send them the details of your inquiries and a copy of the deceased's death certificate so that they could look into the matter of striking his name from the lists.

After making the rounds of the streets, you arrive with your patrol at the head of the bridge. You slow down, then come to a full halt. I'm not far from you. You turn your head, sensing the presence of someone watching you, but you don't see me.

Every time you come here, you can't help but notice the fact that there's no traffic on the bridge. You only find it empty at this time of the night, and distant memories, which you call to mind only hesitantly, are resurrected. It's the perfect place for lovers just now. You used to see them in another time and place, perhaps before you joined the police force. No sooner had the bridge cleared than they would make their appearance. They would stroll in pairs. As you walked along, you would slow down and gawk at them, yet your face wouldn't betray a hint of what was on your mind. The couple would pass by you without even noticing that you existed. Leaning on each other, they would whisper and laugh without making a sound. His hand would envelop hers, and you could see their two hands hanging loosely between them. They would never get as far as the end of the bridge. Instead, they would turn back just before getting there, as though the streets reminded them of what was around them.

During your engagement, you wanted to try it for yourself, and it occurred to you to come out in full uniform, as it would give you a kind of self-assurance and keep at bay the curious stares that make you so furious. Your bride-to-be was enthusiastic about the idea. No sooner had you taken her hand than she surrendered it to you and nestled up against you. The two of you went strolling like the others, and as she whispered to you, her lips grazed your earlobe. She said she wished she could kiss you. She'd never said anything like this before. However, the first thing that occurred to you when you heard it was that she must have come out on a stroll like this before. It didn't appear to be her first time. After all, she was walking just like the other girls, murmuring things to you of the sort you didn't want to hear anymore now that you'd donned a policeman's cap. The others on the bridge stared at you furtively as they walked by. They'd never seen a police uniform in that place before.

The old quarter on the other side is calm, immersed in drowsiness. However, it's a never-ending source of anxiety for you. The inquiries that have been conducted there aren't reassuring. There are troublemakers that never stop inciting unrest, yet nothing you do or say ever lands them in your grip. They're on their guard, and so are you. You're postponing the confrontation. You know it's coming, yet you're not enthusiastic about so-called 'preemptive strikes.' You've received reports to the effect that something is going to happen, possibly within hours. There are no details. However, there's a kind of diffuse rage, and a fierce resentment that's about to lead to an all-out conflagration. That's the most perilous kind. Mindless. The forces at your disposal are sufficient to take care of ordinary situations, but not this type of crisis. It's nighttime, nearly time for the last ritual prayer of the day. You request reinforcements from the central security department, which has a military camp in the desert not far away. No one can see it, and few even know it exists. Yet its camps extend the length of the wadi, a good distance away from populated areas.

Within half an hour the reinforcements have arrived: five vehicles with their large, enclosed beds carrying one hundred soldiers with their gear. You've hidden them behind the police station and they crouch on the ground, the teapots making the rounds among them.

As night approaches you grow increasingly apprehensive. The situation isn't clear. Who might they be? And why are they planning whatever they're planning? You know that the new quarter provokes them through the things they see there and the things they hear about it. However, thus far it's always remained a quiet rage. You also know based on your own study and things that have happened previously in the capital that whenever there's a blow-up, the first thing they do is rush headlong toward the new quarter. And the residents of the new quarter know this as well as you do. Some of them, unlike you, pass such knowledge down among themselves, while others have acquired it as the new quarter has grown increasingly prosperous. You'll always find them ready to take off when danger looms. They have houses in other cities. Their losses won't be great, and they recover them quickly. That isn't what they're worried about. Rather, what worries them is the thought that someone would have the audacity to attack them.

In the old quarter, rage is passed down from one generation to the next. This information is new to you. The rage accumulates over time. All it takes is a tiny spark, and what happens, happens. Calm reigns, buildings are refurbished and repairs are made, and people seem to have regained their serenity. However, it's an illusory serenity of the sort that generally follows on the heels of violence. After all, what's in people's hearts and minds is still there, and things start to build up all over again. On both sides, life is sweet, and there's an alternate intermingling and estrangement.

You don't sleep that night. You stand at the station entrance, listening for some sound to come from the direction of the old quarter. You walk to the head of the bridge and stand there. Nothing. The old quarter has turned out the lights.

It's near midnight. You've never understood it. You've tried, but to no avail. There are six or seven old families of good standing and noble descent who've had connections to agriculture generation after generation. They've never tried anything else. There was a time when their word was influential, respected by all. But now, their influence is a thing of the past, just like that of so many others. What they own is sufficient for them. You talk to them about the profits they might make from another sort of investment and the changes that come with the passing of time. As they listen to you, they pick up some nearby pebbles and roll them a good distance. They don't even comment on what you've said. There are lots of others there, too. You've spoken with them. You try to find things out, and you discover that they don't have anything against the new quarter. Or maybe this is just the way it appears to you. After all, setting fire to two mansions in the new quarter, and on a single night, for that matter, has to mean something.

There's no theft, no attacker. No sign of anything.

One of them says, "Maybe it was the wind."

You look intently into his face, and you can see that he means it. Then he adds, "It happens on our side of the river from time to time. A spark flies. The wind blows up, and something catches on fire. The flames might consume two or three houses."

You nearly tell him that this is different. After all, their houses are right up against each other, they contain a lot of wood, and some of them have fuel, firewood, and various and sundry odds and ends on their roofs. Besides that, most stoves are left lit, either out of absentmindedness or for the heat they provide.

As you're debating with them, you note the fact that the police station has never received a single complaint from their side despite the incidents that take place there. There are fights and numerous injuries. Thefts, too. Yet not a single complaint has ever reached you.

You ask about this and you're told, "There's nothing worth complaining about."

Persisting in your inquiry, you ask whether they solve their problems among themselves.

You're told, "In the end, everybody gets his due."

One day, a sergeant and three soldiers went there on a kind of patrol. They finished their rounds and bought what they wanted from the markets there, then passed by a coffee shop to drink tea and smoke the water pipe before crossing back over the bridge. They tied their horses to the coffee shop window and went in. They filled the water pipe with flavored tobacco once, then a second time, then a third time. A half hour later they came out, and there was no sign of the horses. Everybody knows this sergeant and his antics. You may have heard about him. More than once you've assigned him the job of buying ducks, pigeons, and apples for you to send to your wife in the capital, and he's gotten what he wants for a quarter or half of the price, and sometimes for nothing. In any case, when he'd confirmed the disappearance of the horses, he blew up: he started yelling, then broke a chair, took hold of its back, and threatened the coffee shop proprietor and everybody else there, saying he'd break their heads if the horses didn't reappear in five minutes.

"These are government horses, you bastards!"

Well, the five minutes passed, then still more minutes that seemed like an eternity. He sat there limply on a chair, sweat streaming down his face and his eyes wandering here and there. In the end, the three soldiers who had accompanied him stood him up and led him away. They walked unsteadily across the bridge, which is empty at that time of night. The bags in which they'd placed their purchases hadn't been closed properly, and a number of oranges and tomatoes started falling out of them in succession. The oranges went rolling away at a good clip, whereas the tomatoes—which aren't perfectly round, as you know—were too slow to keep up with them. Then a young chicken jumped out of another bag. Its feet had been bound, so it hopped around, flapping its wings frantically, its squawks ripping through the silence. But not a single one of them turned to look behind him.

They woke you out of your sleep that night. You went to the station wearing your robe over your pajamas and slippers on your feet. You saw the four men coming up the front staircase, but you looked away. You were making preparations at the station for some sort of operation, when suddenly, the sound of neighing rang out through the night, and from the front landing, you glimpsed the four horses trotting lightly over the bridge, confident of the way back to the station.

You return from where you've been standing at the head of the bridge. You cast a glance behind the police station, where the soldiers from central security are sitting. Their eyes glisten in the dark when they turn in your direction.

Heavy with drowsiness, you issue orders for the bridge to be opened and head for your office, where you stretch out on the sofa and sleep securely.

He was in his room on top of the roof, hunched over the model. It still lacked brick kilns in the old quarter. How could he have forgotten them, with their tall smokestacks, their black vents, and successive blasts of smoke?

Dawn was on the horizon. Everyone was still asleep. He, too, doused the light and lay down in bed.

No doubt it had been a nightmare. His hand grasped his throat so tightly he could hardly breathe. Kicking and thrashing, he tried to break free. Their faces nearly touching each other, the inspector hissed, "Now you'll tell me. What is it that makes you loiter around the station?"

"What station?"

"What? Are you playing dumb? The one you're standing in front of."

"I'm in my bed."

"Your bed, you bastard?"

He turned and saw that he was, indeed, in front of the station. It was lit up, but no one was coming in or out.

He loosened his grip on his throat.

"And you follow me around. More than once I've seen you behind me. It's easy to pick out your dirty face from all the rest. And now, you're going to tell me. What's your story?"

"There's no story, and no . . ."

"Hurry up, before I bash in your face."

"It's just that I see . . ."

"What is it that you see?"

"I see what's going on."

"And what's going on?"

Relaxing his grip, he stared him in the face.

"Maybe you're one of them, one of those folks that write in the newspapers, and all of it lies."

He made no reply. Perhaps something in his silence would rescue him from his grip. If he thought even for a moment that he wrote for a newspaper, he might let him go.

The inspector turned to leave. Then he came back and punched him in the face, saying, "If I see you one more time. . . ."

Suddenly he woke up, and found himself clinging to the bed frame, his face right up against it. Feeling the coldness of the iron, he relaxed, panting. His body was spent, he was drenched with sweat, and his mouth was dry. He took a drink from a bottle next to the bed. The morning sun covered the floor of the room. The window. He'd forgotten to close it. And it was time for him to wake up.

He got up sluggishly, running his hand over his throbbing face. In the mirror he saw a red bruise on his upper cheek. He turned around and looked at the bed frame.

Five

It's early morning. The station entranceway has just been washed down and water is dripping off the sides of the steps. You come in hurriedly and, without stopping, ask about the investigations assistant.

You're told that he's waiting for you in your office.

He rises to meet you. You set your cap and baton on a small table and ask him, "Have you prepared the force?"

"Everything's all set."

"Where is it?"

"It's buried beside a tree in the park."

"But the irrigation water may have seeped into it."

"It's wrapped in several plastic bags inside a tin box."

"The same one?"

"The same one."

"Three people with you ought to be enough. I'll get the papers ready for when you come."

"Wait until we've weighed it. I've forgotten how much it weighs. It's been five months."

"Ah, it's been a long time this time. If I hadn't remembered all of a sudden . . ."

"What's happening these days is enough to make a person forget anything."

"Don't remind me of the old quarter. I want to forget all about it today."

"We've been strung out for an entire week now. It just goes on and on. No sooner do things start to settle down enough for us to catch our breath than. . . . We ought to just settle it once and for all. If you're of a different opinion, let me know."

"If it were up to me, I'd invade the old quarter. We'd pull it up by the roots. And someone besides you has had the same idea."

"Who's that?"

"Someone who holds a prominent post. He said in so many words, 'Why don't you set fire to it? That could be arranged.'"

"And I agree with him."

"Don't rush into anything. Caution is in order when dealing with folks like him. What will happen is that you, I, and everyone else here will be the first ones to be sacrificed."

"If you thought this way, you wouldn't do anything."

"Let's stick to the subject at hand. When do you leave?"

"Now."

He got up and stretched a bit, then said, "The central security force. I didn't see it."

"I sent them back last night."

"Might you not have kept them for another two or three days?"

"We could have done that."

The assistant went out.

He mounted the horse with the force behind him, and they set out.

He was following them. The sun was so bright it hurt his eyes. When they reached the park, they tied their horses outside. A small sign on the gate read, "Closed for watering."

They went in. The gardener was on the other side of the park, in his hand a hose with water streaming out of it. He threw it down and came rushing over.

They gathered in a circle around a tree at the edge of the park. The gardener wormed his way in among them.

"Is everything all right, sir?" he asked.

"And since when has everything been all right? Bring something for us to dig with here."

"Dig? I hope everything's all right!"

"Just do what you're told."

"Right."

He rushed away, then came back with a shovel.

"Dig here, beside the root. Easy does it."

In no time the surface of the tin box had appeared, half a meter by a quarter of a meter.

"My heavens!" exclaimed the gardener, retreating.

"Take it out!" commanded the assistant in a stern tone of voice.

"Is it a corpse?"

"What do you mean, a corpse, you numbskull?"

"Corpses are the only things you go digging for."

For this he got a smack on the back of his neck. Not turning around to see where it had come from, he bent down and lifted out the box, then placed it at the assistant's feet.

"Have you been working here for a long time?"

"A little over two years."

"Have you seen this box before?"

"God knows . . ."

"Do you know what's in it?"

"God knows, sir."

"Do you suspect anyone in particular of having put it here?"

"Thousands of folks come in here."

"Come with us to the station where they'll take your deposition."

"Station? God knows . . ."

"Shut up."

"Are you going to put me in jail?"

You and the assistant are in your office, and the tin box sits open in a corner of the room. You get some papers out of a small metal cabinet to the right of the desk. There's a small table between you and the assistant, and you sit down across from him, your heads nearly touching: Statement of rewards for drug confiscation, Khaldiya Police Station.

"First, the reports."

"Let me do them. I've memorized the formula. First, the documentation report: On such-and-such a day in such-and-such a month, and based on a tip supplied by an unnamed informant known to us, two kilograms of hashish were found buried under a tree."

Signatures and a stamp.

He put the paper aside.

"And an examination report: It has become apparent to us, members of the committee formed on orders from the Inspector of the Khaldiya Police Station, that the contraband sequestered on such-and-such a date, in accordance with the data set forth in Sequestration Report No. . . , consists of two kilograms of premium quality hashish which is violent in its effects. The brand name of the aforementioned contraband is known as 'al-A'war,' or, 'Blind Man,' its value comes to 32,000 Egyptian pounds, and it is recommended that it be destroyed."

Signatures and a stamp.

He placed the second paper on the top of the first.

"And a disposal report: On such-and-such a day in such-and-such a month—Should it be the same day? Of course . . .—we, the members of the committee formed in accordance with the decision issued by the Inspector of the Khaldiya Police Station, undertook to destroy the amount of hashish confiscated, the details of which are set forth in Sequestration Report No . . . and the value of which is estimated at 32,000 Egyptian pounds, by setting fire to it out of doors at a site located a good distance from populated areas."

Signatures and a stamp.

He placed the paper on top of the other two.

"And now, the rewards statement."

"Refer to a previous statement as a guide."

"There's no need to refer to a previous one or anything else. Half the value. Sixteen thousand pounds are disbursed to the unnamed informant, and the rest is distributed among the station employees according to their salaries based on the part played by each in the effort expended. There hasn't been any change in the laws since the previous statement, and according to the existing statutes, 'The value of whatever drugs are sequestered is to be distributed in the form of rewards among the members of the sequestration force and those who provide them with assistance.'"

"Nor is there going to be any change. Leave the statement for me to fill out. I'll refer back to the previous one to make sure we don't forget anybody. Take the reports and collect the needed signatures. Take the bag with you for them to see it. Sometimes the chief clerk likes to be exact, so if he wants to change the wording of any of the reports, let him do that."

The assistant absents himself briefly, then comes back. You're engrossed in getting the statement ready.

You ask him, "Did things go well?"

"Perfectly," he replies.

After signing and stamping the statement, you give it to him and he slips it into an envelope with the reports.

"We'll send it today."

You glance at the bag of drugs on your desk. Gesturing toward it you say, "And this?"

"This time I'll find a place for it away out in the desert."

"Will you inform me of it?"

"Of course."

"It would be best to change the box."

"Definitely."

"And now, let's give it a taste."

You reach into the bag and take out a piece half the size of a person's palm and wrapped in cellophane. You sniff it. Then, with an approving nod of the head, you remove an ever so slight amount from the edge of it with your fingernail. You roll it around on your tongue, your eyes half-closed.

"Excellent."

You laugh, and the assistant laughs. You put the piece in an envelope which you stuff into your pocket, and the assistant follows your example. You stare at him in mild astonishment.

"Do you smoke?"

"Not at all, but gifts can do wonders."

"They also diminish the stock on hand. The day's coming when there won't be anything left to confiscate."

"Don't worry. In place of two pieces, I'll bring you ten."

The assistant leaves.

The investigations assistant is a friend of yours. Rebellious and headstrong. To use his own words, he puts all the relevant merchants in his pocket. Coordination is far preferable to confrontation. After all, there's no limit to the harm they can do.

You stand behind the closed window, which is covered by a diaphanous curtain. You like to look out through it. And what do you see? The old lady who sits endlessly on the opposite balcony with a fly swatter in her hand. The minute she hears the creaking of your window as you open it, she turns and eyes you with such exasperation that you end up closing it again.

Your imagination carries you away to the day after tomorrow, when you'll be spending the evening with Hajj Fawzi. A health supplies merchant, he has a number of stores in other cities. In the capital alone he has three. He comes to Khaldiya for three weeks every winter. He says that these three weeks are his entire vacation, the time when he rests from work and family. Of course, he comes from time to time during the rest of the year, too, spends a few days and leaves. He likes get-togethers with friends. Never in your life have you met such a chivalrous, congenial man. Never once have you asked him for a favor but that he's come through for you. He has vast connections, and has done you services such as finding jobs for relatives of yours in the Gulf or in foreign firms that pay high salaries. Your wife herself had been working as a French teacher in a private school, and perhaps you mentioned this to him by coincidence once. Then to your surprise, one day he asked you if you'd like for your wife to be transferred from the school to a job in a foreign research center that pays five times the salary she'd been getting at the school. And this was a great relief to you.

He hosts his dinner parties in the villa's backyard next to a swimming pool that's never been used. It's lined with a soft blue ceramic that he says is Italian. Brittle yellow tree leaves collect in the bottom of the pool, and he forbids the servants to remove them because he likes to look at them when he's sitting outside. The pool is concealed from the view of unwelcome onlookers by a high wall that's covered in its entirety by a huge mural. The painting features young girls sashaying nimbly and gracefully among headstrong steeds poised to leap, their diaphanous garments flowing over their bodies, floating as on air over their beautiful legs, and their raven black hair flying in all directions behind them.

For some reason you're not aware of, the painting reminds you of the young woman in front of the station, her toenails painted and her veil removed to reveal her black hair, a stray lock of which trembles over one side of her forehead. In fact, all sorts of things remind you of her. You've grown accustomed to calling her to mind before you go to sleep. You remove the veil from her head and let her hair fall about her shoulders.

You look into her eyes, but her gaze never softens. Before dozing off, you murmur, "Perhaps if we met again . . . ?" Based on your inquiries about her, you know that she's a primary school teacher, married to a relative of hers who works as an employee at the textile factory. She's been married for a year and a half. The day she came to the station, her brother had been arrested and was among the suspects.

The investigations assistant says with a laugh, "No problem. We'll bring her to the station!"

"How?"

"We arrest her husband for whatever reason, and she'll come after him. You'll have things to say to her, and she'll have things to say to you."

But you don't like the idea at all. You're not comfortable with it. Rather, you have the sense that if the two of you are to meet, it will happen of its own accord.

Noticing that you're drawn to the mural, Hajj Fawzi asks you, "You like it, eh?"

Then he continues, saying, "Yes, it's beautiful. I may have told you all its story before."

Every time we get together he tells the story with the same gusto: "The artist who did the painting never wears anything but shorts, a faded tee-shirt and sandals."

He brought him all the way from Malta. And why Malta? He had gone there for some reason he couldn't remember anymore, and in a shop that specializes in artwork, he saw a small painting that struck his fancy.

"The very same painting that you see before you. They brought out the painter and we made a deal. He was a white boy,

59

skinny, with a pale face and blond dirty hair that came down to his shoulders. I agreed to supply him with a plane ticket, then a first-class train ticket on an air-conditioned coach. However he declined the first-class train ticket, and said he preferred third class on an old-style train. That's what he was in the mood for. So what are you going to say to him? He came carrying a backpack just like the ones kids take to school with them, and in it was everything he needed: painting supplies, a tee-shirt and two changes. He refused to sleep in a room in the mansion but he was delighted with the chaise lounge there in the corner. Do you see it? 'That's all I need,' he said. He slept on it and ate there, too. He was crazy about oranges. He could put away three kilos in a single sitting. Even when he was taking a break and walking here and there, he'd always have an orange in his mouth. He wouldn't peel it. He'd cut a hole in it and suck it. And he refused to let us juice them for him. When I suggested the idea to him, he looked at me as though I'd said something bizarre. Then one day, the oranges happened to run out. We'd been in the habit of putting them in a basket for him beside the chaise lounge. So when they ran out, he looked around him like a kid that's lost his toy, then came charging into the kitchen looking for one. The servants didn't understand what he was saying, and he didn't understand what they were saying. After that, they figured out what he wanted, and one of them ordered some for him over the phone. The amount originally agreed upon had been one or two kilos a day. As long as he was around, we needed a crateful every day. It was fun to watch him. Whenever I had a free minute, I'd pull a chair up to the window on the second floor and look down at him. I was careful not to let him see me though, for fear that he might get stressed. I've heard that artists don't like people watching them on the sly. They get irritated and edgy. They might even scratch out the painting and take off. He would work half-naked. Yeah. With nothing but his shorts on. Day and night he'd be on top of the ladder, so we brought him a good flashlight. The three maids in the villa were crazy about him. They'd hide somewhere and watch him, then rush in to wash whatever changes of clothes or paraphernalia he happened to throw down. They'd stand beside the chaise lounge while he was eating, just waiting for a sign from him. Sometimes I'd have to call them several times when I needed something, and after my voice had gone hoarse, one of them would finally show up and say, 'You called, sir? We were cleaning!'

"The youngest of them, I don't remember her name, was the most enthralled with the boy. He'd be sitting on the chaise lounge taking a break and she'd take hold of a wet towel. Then, without asking his permission, and without saying a word—since even if she had said something, he wouldn't have understood her—she'd lean down over him and clean his dirty torso. The boy didn't take a bath the entire time he was here, not even in the mornings. Instead, he would just take a wet towel and wipe his face and underarms. Maybe the girl got the idea from seeing him do that. She'd clean his back, his neck and his chest, and the boy would just laugh and let her have her way with him. The other two girls stood steadfastly nearby, fretful, their hands on their chests. A few days later, the girl decided she was going to give the boy her virginity. The other two tried to talk her out of it, but it was no use. When they saw how determined she was, they got rid of all the hair on her body: her legs, her arms, her underarms, and her private parts. By the time they had finished with her, she sparkled. She took a bath, did her hair and put on a couple of drops of perfume from a bottle one of the girls used to keep stashed away. Then off she went, entrusting her fate to the Almighty. Her two coworkers stayed in their room, watchful and waiting. They told me about it later, before I fired them. The girl burst in to where the boy was sleeping on the chaise lounge, and ravished him. That's right! It was quite a story. By the next morning, she'd disappeared. We looked all over, but didn't find her. I informed her family, who looked among their relatives and acquaintances, but there was no trace of her. The other two girls were hiding her somewhere in the villa. Then at night, she would slip in to where the boy was. Things went on this way for three weeks, and I didn't have a clue. The boy finished the painting, then waited for a day so that he could get a good look at it. But it was entirely by chance that she fell into my hands.

"It was daybreak, and she was coming back after being with the boy. I was in the outer room. I don't remember what had led me to stay up that night, or what I was doing there. In any case, I heard the sound of the glass door that leads out to the swimming pool. This door. And I saw her dashing toward the kitchen. If she'd looked my way, she would have seen me. She'd lifted up the bottom of her jilbab a bit so that it wouldn't hinder her movement. Taken by surprise, I called out to her. She froze in place. She didn't move a muscle. One minute passed, then two. Then she turned around, trembling, quaking, absolutely terrified. Then I found myself walking toward her. She collapsed at my feet.

"'Forgive me, sir!'

"'Forgive you?'

"All she said was that she'd slept with the boy, and that it was all her fault. She was the one who'd gone to him. She was looking away from me and I couldn't see her face. It took me a while to comprehend what she was saying.

"I told her I was going to send her home to her family for them to deal with her.

"'They'll kill me, sir.'

"'And that's what you deserve.'

"'I'll kill myself, then.'

"These people! I can't figure them out!

"I told her she could do whatever she wanted to herself, as long as it was far from here.

"'Yes, sir,' she said. 'He's leaving in the morning, and I'll leave, too.'

"Then I left her alone. After all, what business is all this of mine? And I went up to my room.

"The next morning I met up with the boy, who was waiting for me, his backpack on his back and ready for departure. He looked around him, then nearly said something, but didn't. Instead, he just gazed at me with a questioning look in his eye.

"I gave him the rest of what I owed him, and told the driver to take him to the train station. As for the girl, we didn't hear a thing about her. And the painting is as you can see. He put his signature on its edge."

It's a long story, and in order to stave off the comments that people are prone to repeat over and over, you get up unexpectedly, laughing, and shout, "I think we need a little something to drink!"

The place is filled with the aroma of grilled meat. Grilled lamb, to be exact. They season it and roast it in a way that gives it a flavor that's out of this world. Two of the servants dress up like the waiters who work in the big restaurants in the capital, with a white jacket, a black bowtie, and light white gloves. One of them is behind the grill and the other is behind the beverage table. Hajj Fawzi is wearing a robe over his pajamas and slippers on his feet. All together, there are nine people in attendance, including the governorate secretary, the head of the city council, three people who always accompany Hajj Fawzi, and two proprietors of neighboring shops. Hajj Fawzi takes a piece out of his pocket. It's half the size of the piece you have with you. He tosses it onto the table around which you all are seated. The bowls mounted atop the water pipe are filled with flavored tobacco and arranged in layers on a holding device. Seven layers, each of which contains sixty bowls. The water pipe is set atop another holding device, and the stove is next to it. As soon as Hajj Fawzi gets to the thirtieth bowl, he starts cracking jokes that have you all doubled over with laughter. He chuckles slightly himself, reveling in the sight of you cutting loose and staggering to and fro, leaning on each other for support and gesturing to him breathlessly to wait a bit before he goes on.

Day after tomorrow will be your surprise. You'll take the piece out of your pocket and toss it into the table, saying "This time, government hashish!"

It's a witty phrase, and the first person to laugh will be the governorate secretary, who'll also cast you a reproachful glance. More than once he's asked you to count him in, and when you leave you're going to pretend to forget what's left of the piece, which will be more than half of it. You'll leave without taking any notice of it even if Hajj Fawzi reminds you to take it with you, and you'll be on your way as if you didn't hear him.

After completing the drug confiscation awards statement, he folded it up, put it in an envelope, and slipped it into the pocket of his coat, which hung on a nail behind the door to his room so that he wouldn't forget it the next morning.

It was past midnight and the roof was empty. He was so weary, he wouldn't be able to take a short stroll the way he usually did, lean against the rooftop wall and look down from his elevated perch until he was overcome with drowsiness. The awards statement had exhausted him, and had taken him longer than the payroll.

He cast a final glance at the model, turned out the light and lay down in bed.

Moonlight flooded the room. As usual, he'd forgotten to close the window, and he turned his face toward the wall to avoid the light.

It's the final hours of the night, the time when activity at the station is usually at its ebb. The officer on duty has brought a comfy chair and placed it behind a desk facing the open door. He's also got a strong cup of tea and old magazines that he pulled out of the desk drawer to help keep him awake. He unbuttons his jacket and relaxes into his seat.

He isn't far away. He's coming from the bridge, and stops hesitantly in front of the station's lighted entrance. He comes slowly up the staircase, but on the third step, he's surprised to find that the inspector has arrived. His voice going before him, the inspector addresses whoever is with him in an angry tone. He ascends the stairs in a hurry, then before he reaches the final step, he stops and turns toward him.

"You again," he says. "I warned you!"

Having said this, he gives him a violent shove that sends him rolling to the ground.

The morning light was in his eyes, and the chill of the tile floor was coursing through his cheek. He was sprawled out on the floor near the bed. In the course of his fall, he had pulled the light blanket down with him, and it was wrapped around his legs. How many times had he reminded himself to get a rug to cover the floor of the room? His feet couldn't take the dampness. And the tile wasn't even nice to look at. It was a dull gray and had holes in it here and there. His nose hurt, and there was dried blood on his moustache. He must have fallen on his face. But how could the pain have failed to wake him up? Bleeding a bit, he moved away from the mirror.

Six

She ravished him!

He raised his eyebrows slightly the way he did whenever he was taken aback.

It was Friday, his day off, and he slept in for a long time. The sun was bright and warm.

If only he could see her again . . .

He turned toward the model. A subtle smile appeared at the corners of his mouth, then vanished.

She wasn't more than sixteen years old. She wore her hair in a black braid that was slender like her neck. She stood concealed in a dark corner, watching the boy as he sat on the ladder, which was fitted out with wheels so that he could move it easily back and forth. With a bright flashlight to see by, he held one paintbrush between his teeth and one in his hand. His naked torso was soiled all over, and bits and pieces of tree leaves clung to the hair on his golden head. If he had let her, she would have bathed him and massaged his body not just once, but twice. And once she'd gotten through with him, he wouldn't have even recognized himself. With her hand she suppressed a giggle that nearly escaped as she imagined him standing there in disbelief after a bath. She searched his bag when he was looking the other way, but didn't find a thing. Just two changes, one of which was dirty. He leaned over the painting, balancing himself on his toes. She held her breath, panting, for fear that the ladder might move and send him tumbling. She kept vigil in her dark corner until he had finished. He wiped his hands and his face on a piece of cloth that he threw onto the ladder. He turned out the light, then lay down with a groan on the chaise lounge. She stayed seated where she was until he had gone to sleep, after which it would have been time for her to head for her own bed.

But instead, she ravished him!

Under the light of the stars, the darkness tranquil, he lay on his back looking at her, and she at him. She lay down beside him, placed her hand on his chest and pressed her face to his cheek. She pulled her jilbab up, raised her bare leg, and brought it down cautiously on top of his outstretched leg. Then she grew still, her breaths coming in rapid succession. She felt his hand unbuttoning his shorts. She helped him to pull them down, then mounted him. She stayed on top of him even after they'd both finished. He smiled at her gently, caressed her cheek with his fingers, then closed his eyes. She was still on top of him as drowsiness began to take him far away. Then she felt his body move under her, and she understood that she should get up. With the edge of her jilbab, she wiped off the blood that had flowed from her body onto his. She buttoned up his shorts, then looked around in search of a sheet to cover him with. She didn't find one. She sat beside the chaise lounge looking at him. His breathing was calm and his lips parted. A strand of his hair had settled on his cheek and over the side of his eye. She nearly brushed it aside, but then thought better of it, fearing she might wake him up.

He stood in front of the model with his head bowed and his hands behind his back. Then suddenly he was wakened out of his reverie by the sound of his neighbor coming up the stairs. Through the open window he could see her carrying two folded-up rugs on her head and a feather duster in her hand. She walked along the edge of the roof and lopped the two rugs over the wall. Before she turned around, he'd closed the door and lain down again.

She opened the door and stood in the doorway.

"So you stay home even on your day off?"

Looking around the room, she continued, "Not even a refrigerator. Who can do without one these days? Give me a drink out of the jug. My mouth is dry."

He brought her the jug and a cup. Contenting herself with the jug, she took two swigs, then gave it back to him. Noticing the model on the desk, she laughed.

"Are you playing? Amusing yourself?"

Standing a couple of steps away, he looked at her without saying a word.

"What's wrong? Did I say something to upset you?"

She looked at him for a long time with a smile on her face, leaning with her palm against the doorframe. Then she plunged her hand into the neck opening of her jilbab.

"Look. If you come near me, I'll scream."

He went on looking at her without saying a word. It terrified him to think of her doing that and screaming without his even having come near her. Staring at him out of the corner of her eye, she shook out her jilbab with her hand and left.

This time he latched the door from the inside, then lay down again.

After nightfall, he went out, thinking to himself: Maybe I'll meet up with Younis. And he did.

Younis came into the coffee shop in his usual rowdy way, greeting everyone, then sat down beside him.

They had their drinks in silence, then Younis asked him with a laugh, "Won't there be another check soon?"

He looked at him questioningly.

Laughing again, Younis said, "Really! Expenses are adding up!"

He leaned over and steadied the hot embers on top of the water pipe.

"My neighbor upstairs—the one I told you about—her name is Nowsa. She eats a lot."

"She's still with you?"

"If she'd found somebody better than me, she'd have left me and settled down by now."

"What makes you stay with her?"

"What makes me stay with her? She's a whore, that's for sure. But she's pretty. Great body. Great sense of humor. Everything. I used to always dream of having a woman like her. My wife is too respectable in everything."

He tapped his feet together, drying the tears that had flowed while he was laughing.

"If I weren't afraid she'd throw herself at you, I'd take you with me to see her. The problem with her is that she eats too much. She's got a stomach of iron. And all she wants is the most expensive things: plums, apples, you know. She can eat an entire kilo. And of a whole kilo of kebab that I take with me, all I get is a couple of pieces. The other day, she asked for mangoes. 'And where am I supposed to get mangoes?' I asked her. 'It's a long time till mango season.' 'That's what I'm in the mood for,' she said. 'Tell yourself to have a little patience.' 'Seriously. I want them.' I had my head on her bare arm, soft and nice as can be, and I wasn't in the mood for conversation. But what could I do? I looked up at her. She smiled and said, 'Ah-hah! I might be having cravings!'

"Well, when I heard that, I nearly jumped out of my skin. She was running her fingers through my hair, and I hid my face under her arm. She said, 'It hasn't come for the last two months.'

"What? The water?"

"'No, my period. Didn't you ask me once if there was anything you could get for me?'

"It's true that I'd said that to her. But it had just been talk."

"I told her, 'I'll find you some mango if I have to go to the ends of the earth.'

"Meanwhile I thought: Oh my God! That had never even occurred to me! What are you doing, Younis? The next time she came, she went into the bedroom with me behind her, and took off her jilbab. She always wears a black slip, since she knows that's what I like the most. In any case, I asked her to dance a little bit before her tummy gets big. She jiggled her middle a bit, then said, 'Let's sleep first.' 'Before we sleep, and after.' 'OK, let me think it over.'

"She often used to dance in the bedroom while I tapped my finger on the side of the bed. I brought a long scarf to tie around her hips, and she spread out her arms and waited.

"'On the table,' I said.

"'No, here.'

"'Just once I'd like to see you do it on the table, with the light shining down on you.'

"It's a medium-sized dining table in the living room, round, with four legs. One of them had come off and I'd held it in place with a small nail until we could get it repaired. When she saw the table she said, 'Will it hold me?'

"'It would hold three of you.'

I held onto the table with one hand on the side where the loose leg was, and put my other hand on her back to help her keep her balance. Supporting herself on my shoulder and with one foot on the chair, she stepped up onto the table with the other. Then she stood up straight and took a deep breath. I let go of the edge of the table to tap on the top of it, and after just one or two jiggles, she took a spill. I thought she'd died. She lay there on her back, not moving a muscle, and her face was yellow as a lemon. I panicked. You bet. Big time. I put her head on my arm and said, 'Nowsa! Answer me! Nowsa!' I went and got some cologne and held it up to her nose. After a while she opened her eyes. With me supporting her and her holding her back, we made it over to the bed. She just stared at me without saying a word. She let me massage her cheeks and her neck with cologne, but didn't take her eyes off me. Ah,

I understand. A woman like her, I should have understood. I thought she wouldn't be back after that. But one day passed, then another, and back she came. And there was no more talk about cravings or mangoes. I left the table leaning on its side. She sees it every time she comes and conceals a smile. Women! What were we saying? Oh, yeah. I was asking if there would be another check soon."

"There may be one in a few days."

"You told me to call you Mr. Salem?"

"That's right. Any objections?"

"No, not at all. I was just refreshing my memory."

His hands clasped under his potbelly, he looked out of the corner of his eye at the water pipe bowl, where a layer of ashes had formed on top of the live embers.

He said, "The bowl. Shall I order you another one?"

"No need. Let's go."

And they left.

They walked in the semi-darkness down a broad side street. There were few people out and about.

"The streets are different at night than they are during the day," said Younis.

The other made no comment.

"Why didn't you bring your cane?"

"I forgot it. By the way, I want to ask you about something."

"Go right ahead."

"Do you know the people around here? On this street, for example?"

"I know most of them. I've lived in this neighborhood since I was a kid."

"All right. How about the most unfortunate family here?"

"The most unfortunate?"

Younis stopped and stared at him.

"So you want to help them?"

"Something like that."

Gripped with a sudden enthusiasm, Younis looked around him.

"Yes! Yes! It'll be the best thing you've ever done in your life! We just passed it."

"What?"

"Their house. Over there. The third corner on the left."

"Who are they?"

"A mother and three children. When she couldn't make ends meet anymore, she pulled them out of school so that they could work. Her husband worked in a factory, smelting iron or lathing, I don't remember which. Anyway, he died. The machine ate him up. She got no compensation or damages. The factory proprietors and officials said it was his fault. They issued her a certain amount as aid which kept her going for two or three months. His coworkers took up a collection for her, and promised to give her the same amount on the first of every month. That continued for six months, then the amount started to dwindle from one month to the next until it stopped coming altogether."

"How old is she?"

"Fifty, I'd say."

"And how old are her children?"

"The oldest is a girl. I'd guess she's about. . . . That's right, she's my daughter's age. There's a difference of two or three months between them, but I don't remember which one is older."

74

They entered a narrow alleyway, where they saw a light in a ground-floor window covered with thin iron bars. Younis pointed to it, and nearly rushed to the door. The other held him back.

"Wait," he said. Then, taking a sealed envelope out of his coat pocket, he whispered, "Calm down."

"I'm calm, I'm calm," he replied.

Still excited, he looked at the window, then back at the envelope in the other's hand.

"Before they go to sleep," he whispered impatiently. "Once they've turned out the lights, they won't see the envelope."

"Here. Slip it between the bars, but without making a sound."

"I got it, I got it."

He rushed over to the window, but when he got closer, he discovered that he couldn't quite reach it. He looked around in search of a large rock.

"A rock would do the trick," he whispered. "Just a rock. But where can we get one? There has to be one somewhere around here . . ."

The other stepped lightly up to the window.

"Support yourself on my shoulder," he whispered.

Younis rested a hand on his shoulder, then thrust his body upward and dropped the envelope between the bars. The minute they heard the sound of it hitting the floor, they dashed away and hid in the entranceway to a nearby house.

Before long, voices could be heard coming from inside the house: Gasps. Screams. Shouts. Someone climbed up to the window from the inside, and the face of a shirtless young boy could be seen as he tried to slip between two bars, looking to the right, then to the left. They heard a door open, and a woman came rushing out barefoot. She stood on the sidewalk in front of the house, looking around and shouting, "Who is it? Who is it?"

She was wearing a light jilbab whose neck opening she drew closed with her hand, and her hair hung down loosely.

"Who is it?" she asked again, her voice suddenly growing fainter.

Then, holding onto the wall for support, she collapsed.

Younis nearly rushed over to her, but the other held him back. A boy and girl came out of the house, grasped her under her arms and tried to lift her up.

She looked at them and murmured, "I was wondering where you were. He's gone. I couldn't catch up with him."

Nearby windows and balconies lit up while voices called out "What is it, Umm Ahmad? Is everything all right?"

"Everything's all right," she replied in a feeble voice as she surrendered to her son and daughter and went back into the house.

Within moments the lights had gone out, and the alleyway went dark again.

Emerging from their hiding place, they walked to the main street.

"How much money did you put in the envelope?" asked Younis, drying his eyes.

"Well, uh . . ."

"You're right. It isn't proper for me to ask. But after what we've seen, I hope it wasn't less than a thousand."

"Tell me when you hear about others."

"For sure. For sure."

Then suddenly he stopped in his tracks again. "Ah! I don't know. Maybe . . ."

The other looked at him questioningly.

"Do you have another envelope with you?" Younis asked.

"Yes, I do. Who is it?"

"You might not agree with me. You might get angry with me."

"Who?"

"A woman. Two corners down. She lives in a room on the ground floor. She used to work in a nightclub. You know, a long time ago. Then she got old and went to work in taverns. What did she do there? She might have been a cleaning lady. In any case, she ended up here. She comes out late at night and does the rounds of the restaurants and bars, where some people give her something to eat or drink."

He fell silent, looking at the other out of the corner of his eye as they walked.

"You said it was two corners down. Where, exactly?"

"Now you're talking!"

"They entered a blind alley. The house was dark, as was its entranceway. However, there was light stealing out from under the door. Younis knocked gently.

"Madame Siham?"

"Yes. Who is it?"

Younis turned and said in a whisper, "It's her."

The other gave him the envelope and he slipped it under the door, then they hurried off and hid in an alleyway entrance.

They heard a door open and saw her rush outside. She stood in front of the house wearing pajama trousers and a short-sleeved shirt. She looked right and left with the envelope in her hand.

Then she went back into her room.

They were just about to leave the alley when they saw her come out again. This time she had put a shawl over her shoulders and some thongs on her feet. When she passed in front of them, they also saw what appeared to be a dark-colored bow in her silver hair.

She walked with a straight posture, and they walked behind her, keeping themselves hidden behind this wall and that. They came out onto the main street and she kept going. Then, three corners later, she crossed to the other side of the street.

A large grocery store was still open, and she disappeared inside.

She came out carrying a paper bag that she hugged to her chest and a long loaf of Italian bread in her hand. When she passed them, they glimpsed the mouths of three glass bottles peeking out of the bag. As they walked behind her, Younis whispered, "I thought. . . . It never occurred to me. You have every right to be angry with me."

"Be angry with you?"

"For leading you to her."

"What was wrong with that?"

She stopped in front of her house and turned to look at the houses opposite her, from the top floor to the bottom, muttering, "You sons of bitches."

Then her voice started to get louder, and louder.

"Sons of bitches. Sons of bitches!"

A number of windows and balconies lit up, scattering the darkness of the alleyway. Meanwhile, she stood in the middle of the lane shouting nonstop, "Tell them! Tell them!"

The shawl fell off her shoulders and clung to one of her feet, and she drew it along with her as she stumbled forward. The bag slipped out of her grip, and as it fell, there rang out the sound of shattering glass. She took no notice of the broken bottles at first, but when she did, she struck the empty-looking bag with her foot. Screaming and waving her arms with the loaf of bread still in her hand, she moved away from the house, then fell on her face. She kicked her feet a couple of times, then her body grew still.

Someone ran over to her.

Meanwhile, the two men emerged from the alleyway and walked down the main street.

"Did she die?" whispered Younis.

He heard no reply. And when they reached Younis's house, they parted.

Seven

He stood on the bridge looking out at the river, leaning his elbows on the railing.

He'd taken a tour of the old quarter. He lingered in the streets and alleyways and ventured into the congested markets, where he found the women to be the fiercest bargainers. Here and there scuffles would break out and reach their climax: fistfights and the tearing of clothes—then die down again of their own accord. Half-naked children ran around in a flock, making their way through the press of legs. Drawn to the small puddles in the market, they went around imitating the sound of a choo-choo train, splashing water on some of the passersby and oblivious to the flood of invectives and curses they brought on themselves and their families.

He glimpsed a transport vehicle parked in the shade of some trees on the side of the road. Seated under the trees were two boys, neither of whom could have been more than four years old. They were sitting right up next to each other, and one of them had his arm around the other's shoulder. They had a piece of cake which they'd gotten somehow or other from the nearby bakery. As if they were afraid it would disappear too quickly, each of them would take a bit of it on the tip of his finger, savor it slowly, then take another bit. And throughout, each of them kept both eyes on the other's finger. If he had waited a bit longer, he would have seen them exercise increasing restraint as the piece was about to run out.

He wanted to see her house from up close, the house of the woman with the painted toenails. And he did see it. It was a white, two-story building which, until just recently, had been one story only, with concrete pillars rising over its roof in anticipation of the son's marriage. And now he could see the pillars stretching upward over the roof of the second story in anticipation of the marriage of the as-yet unborn grandson. Outside its small balcony there were clotheslines with multicolored clothespins hanging from them. If she would only appear now! As he stood at the head of the side street, she made her appearance. She was carrying a large tub of clean laundry. She wrung out a piece for the last time and a few drops of water fell onto the street. She shook out each item and hung it on the line. Two shirts and a pair of men's pajamas. Then she stood up straight again. With her face to the setting sun and her braided hair glistening with moisture, she wore a light, collarless short-sleeved jilbab that revealed her slightly rounded neck.

Footsteps were approaching, but he didn't turn around. He was too busy gazing into the river with its gentle undulations.

"You?"

Decked out in full uniform, the inspector stood two steps away from him, thumping the side of his pants with his small billy club. The bridge was empty. There was no one but the two of them.

Looking at him in amazement, the inspector said, "You baffle me. What's your story? You came to mind yesterday and I thought: Maybe he's hiding himself somewhere and keeping track of my every move. You don't know what it's like for there to be somebody behind you who's got his eye on you every minute, watching your every step. Are you enjoying yourself? I was sure I'd meet up with you tonight. I've started to get fed up with you. And always in that overcoat. You must sleep in the thing! It smells like piss. Donkey piss! What's your story? If what you're after is a scoop for your newspaper, then come to my office the way respectable folks do. You'll drink your coffee and I'll tell you enough to fill your newspaper for a whole year. How much do they pay you?"

He fell silent, looking in the direction of the old quarter.

Then he continued, "They've informed me that you were there. Come on, let's walk a while and talk."

He didn't budge from where he was standing.

The inspector went on, "It upsets me to talk to somebody and to have this somebody not answer me. I get angry. Do you hear me? I get angry. And my anger isn't an easy thing."

As the inspector spoke, the other came up and stood beside him, placing his elbows on the railing as he himself had been doing.

"There's something mysterious about you that I'm not comfortable with. Not comfortable at all. And what do you see here? The river. The water in the river. You may have seen some fish jumping."

He laughed. "Yes, they jump in an arc, their fins erect, and their silver color shimmers. Then somebody shouts, 'They're so beautiful! They're so marvelous!' They stand there when the fish are being roasted, savoring their aroma and saying, 'It smells delicious.' Then they devour it like nobody's business. You know? I, for example, can't stand to see them slaughtering pigeons, and if I happen to see them by accident, I won't go near them when somebody's eating them in spite of the fact that I love them. Really. They're so beautiful! They're so marvelous! And that can tell you a lot about other things, too. Ask me. The worst place in the world to work is a police station. All sorts of people are dumped into my lap, and every sort of catastrophe you can imagine. You want to write? Write, then. I've got a story for you. All right. Get this: one story. Just one. A first-class businessman. Contracting deals. Cashmere overcoats. Wool tunics and silk kufiyehs. A 24-carat ring the size of an egg on his finger, so big it tilts to one side. Groomed perfectly. The latest fashions. If he runs into anybody who's had hard luck, he reaches into his pocket and gives him something. Beggars and non-beggars alike. In fact, he's happy when he sees them running to him. He comes into the coffee shop, and before you know it, there are orders for all the customers at his expense. There in the old quarter, the disaster area. Fine. So far, so good. Let come what will. I come into the station and see him standing in front of the lieutenant. With him is a seventeen-year-old girl wearing an old jilbab, a veil on her head and thongs on her feet. Her belly is distended. She's his daughter by a woman he's divorced.

"The lieutenant asks her, 'Who did this to you, girl?'

"'My father, sir.'

"The businessman mutters, 'Don't believe her, sir.'

"His plump cheeks are shaved clean, his moustache looks perfect, and he smells of cologne. I think to myself: Even when you come to the police station?

"Anyway, they'd called him in based on a complaint from the girl. A woman I hadn't seen when I first came in was huddled in a corner next to the door. Her black jilbab, her veil, and her head were all covered with dirt. She wailed and moaned, her body swaying back and forth.

"'He did it, sir, he did it.'

"She started to get up and the lieutenant shouted at her, 'Stay where you are!'

"After taking a couple of sips of tea, he turned to the girl.

"'Tell your story.'

"'He divorced my mother.'

"'The woman who's sitting and moaning at the door?'

"'Yes. A few months ago, his second wife got mad at him and went back to her family, and he and I were alone in the house. I used to say: Shall I go stay with Mom, Dad?'

"The businessman screeched, 'And her husband who's with her? Or is it you that wants it? Does he hit you, or does he do something else? You're just like your mother!'

"The lieutenant asked, 'Did your mother's husband do this?'

"'Do what, sir? No! He's simple and kindhearted.'

"'Go on.'

"'I sweep the house, wash his clothes and cook rich dishes for him every day till I'm all tired out. One night he came home late, the way he usually does. I heard him talking gibberish and I knew he'd been drinking. When he drinks, I'm afraid of him.'

"'Why are you afraid?"

"'He looks at me in a bad way.'

"'What does he drink?'

"'I don't know. Ask him.'

"'Does he do things other than drink?'

"'Opium. He's always got a piece under his tongue.'

"'Don't believe her, sir. This is just a story she's cooked up with her mother.'

"'Quiet!' shouted the lieutenant.

"Then, turning to the girl, he said, 'Go on.'

"'He came in to where I was, and I found him at my head. I didn't have time to cover my legs.'

"She fell silent, her face stony and her eyes motionless.

"The businessman mumbled, 'Don't believe her, sir.'

"The lieutenant threw the pen that was in his hand.

"'I told you to be quiet!'

"Then all of a sudden he got up, raging, and struck him with his palm. As for the businessman, he acted as though no one had hit him. Instead, he just took the slap, his cheek quivered momentarily, and that was that.

"The lieutenant asked the girl, 'And you? Didn't you scream? Or run?'

"'How could I have screamed or run, sir? His hand was on my neck, and he was biting me.'

"'Biting you?'

"'Yes. He bit my face.'

"'And what happened after that?'

"'What do you mean, after that, sir?'

"'After he did what he did, didn't you go to your mother? Leave the house?'

"'After what happened, where could I go, sir?'

"'And did he sleep with you again?'

"'Again and again. Every night, except for Wednesdays and Saturdays.'

"'Why Wednesdays and Saturdays?'

"'He stays up all night with gentlemen friends of his.'

"'What "gentlemen"?'

"'He says they bring him work.'

"Turning to the businessman, the lieutenant said, 'So you're think you're some sort of stud, you good-for-nothing. . . . Every night?'

"'And you believe her about this, too, sir?'

"Turning back to the girl, the lieutenant asked, 'Did he used to threaten you?'

"'Sometimes he'd threaten me. He'd tell me he was going to kill me. And other times . . .'

"She fell silent and looked at the lieutenant.

"'And other times . . . ?' he asked.

"'Other times he'd tell me he was going to marry me off to somebody, and that he was going to buy me dresses, glass bracelets and bangles.'

"'Did he buy them for you?'

"'No.'

"'And you're complaining now?'

"'My stomach's gotten big and it shows. They'll kill me.'

"'Who?'

"'He, or somebody else.'

"'Who else, besides him?'

"'Somebody associated with him. Or with my mother. For sure . . .'

"I stood aside and didn't intervene in the interrogation. Instead, I moved away. When I looked at the man, I thought to myself: He might do a thing like that. But when I'd gotten away from him, I couldn't believe he would have done such a thing. I thought: surely the girl must be in cahoots with her mother. But whether he did it or not, that's not my point. Do you understand? What's going on? This is just one of thousands of stories. And who would believe that I'm standing here now beside you and telling you all this? A few days ago, I hit you. Yet you still haven't told me why you're following me. I don't believe you write for any newspaper. I'm the one who said that, but you've neither confirmed it nor denied it. And now, you hold your tongue. I haven't heard a single word from you. They've seen you in the old quarter. What were you doing there?"

He turned toward him, resting one elbow on the railing.

"Might you be planning something? You're the stranger, the external element that usually comes along to stir things up. I've never seen your face before. You've got no relatives or friends there. Those who've been keeping an eye on you say you haven't taken sides. You haven't even spoken with anyone. So as you can see, the results of the inquiries are in your favor so far. However, inquiries aren't everything. Their results are often inaccurate. We could bring you into the station with the greatest of ease, and after a good thrashing, you'd talk. But I prefer to wait. I have a feeling whatever's cooking isn't done yet, and I want to see what you're up to. It might be something new. In fact, I'll be disappointed if it turns out to be something trivial and old hat. I've been here seven years. The first instructions I ever received were: The old quarter— don't think lightly of it. The old quarter causes them worry in the capital that I didn't understand at first. But now I feel the same unease. It's closed to the outside world. Secretive. It doesn't give out the least bit of information. They have other sources besides me that I know nothing about. They take me by surprise by telling me about things I've never seen or heard of before, and later I discover that they were right. And maybe you're one of their sources?"

He gazed at him wordlessly for a moment, then continued, "You wouldn't tell me, of course. They say the old quarter is on the brink of disaster. And if you're one of their sources, you'll know more than I do. It's due to blow up any minute. When that happens, the first thing they'll do is to rush into the new quarter, and it will mean wholesale destruction. It's an old story that repeats itself every now and then. What's new? Tell me if you're one of them. Just a tiny spark, and the whole place will go up in flames. Fine. I know that without anybody telling me so. It goes without saying. General knowledge. What I want is specifics. Let them supply me with those, and I'll know what action to take. Might you be that spark?"

He eyed him up and down for a few moments, then went on, "And why wouldn't you be? Have you ever in your whole life heard of a police inspector who goes out on patrol? Well, I do.

The lieutenant does the regular patrol in the old quarter. But I'm not content with that. I see for myself. I get my own sense of things, experience things first-hand. I see what he doesn't see. And you?"

He looked at him intently without saying a word.

"From the time they informed me of your presence there, I've had you on the brain. I recall the times when I've seen you. I try to find a suitable category for you, and I see that you might fit in any number of them. What were you doing at her house? Don't pretend as though you don't hear me. She was there on the balcony right in front of you, and the two of you exchanged signals. Have you known her for a long time? Your silence has started to irritate me. Are you an old lover of hers? Now you're making me mad. I can't stand for someone not to answer me when I ask him a question."

As he pulled himself up to his full height, his baton fell and he bent down to pick it up. Perhaps the thought occurred to him when he bent down and saw the dingy old shoes and the feet held close together. Whatever the case may be, he wrapped his arm around the two legs and thrust them violently upward. Then he saw the body double over and plunge headlong into the murky waters below.

He turned and walked with measured steps in the direction of the new quarter.

As he hurtled downward, what he dreaded was the moment when he hit the surface of the water. He awaited it with his heart throbbing. But when it came, he hardly felt it. Instead, he plunged beneath the surface. If he'd only endured a little longer. After all, he was good at staying afloat. Gasping, he looked around him. The bathroom floor was flooded. He was lying on his side, and the water was up to his mouth and his nose. Glimpsing the arc of water pouring out of the rinser inside the toilet, he crawled over to it. Its control device was damaged. He lowered the toilet cover to keep the water inside. He sometimes happened to go into the bathroom while he was asleep, and he may have slipped on the wet floor. He ran his hand over the back of his head and found a tumor-like bump. Had he fainted? And how long had he been lying there? He took off his sopping clothes, wrung them out and lopped them over his arm, then went to hang them out on the line. It was only when he felt the sting of the cold wind on top of the roof that he noticed he wasn't wearing anything, whereupon he beat a quick retreat and shut the door.

He stood in front of the model, thinking about preparing a rewards statement. But rewards for what? Confiscation? Confiscation of what? Drugs? He'd prepared a rewards statement for that only recently. Maintenance of law and order? Law and order are always maintained. He didn't have much interest in visits by officials and the rewards generally granted for that sort of occasion: ten days' salary. Half a month. It wasn't worth the trouble it would take to get the statement ready. In the end, he shoved the papers aside.

A city like Khaldiya needs to be lit up at night, he thought. He picked up a plastic bag filled with things he'd bought on his way home from work. They included an electrical wire with tiny colored light bulbs attached to it: blue, red, transparent, yellow, green, each of them the size of a fava bean. He passed the wire inside the model.

The old quarter: The lights there are few and far between. Most of its remaining street lights are out, their bulbs either damaged or stolen, and with no replacements on their way. As for the poles themselves, some of them have fallen down and are lying on the ground surrounded by accumulations of garbage deposited by the wind. They serve as good resting places for dogs weary of loitering. Others have been pulled up and removed given their usefulness in drainage canals. It's only the old-time kerosene lamps that still hang at the street corners, dimmed out and dusty. And who would have paid any attention to them, anyway?

The statue also remains in place, unwavering in the face of the desires to vandalize and steal. It's the statue of the unknown soldier that stands at the entrance to the old quarter atop a marble base. Residents of the old quarter erected it long ago at their own expense in memory of their sons who had been led away to fight in a war that had nothing to do with them, one hundred and twenty, none of whom returned. The lighting here should be an ashen yellow. For the bridge, transparent light bulbs: Powerful lighting so that you, Mr. Inspector, and those with you can see from a distance everything that creeps or crawls over it.

As for the new quarter, it's a festival of lights: lights of all colors. They really get into lights over there. They hang them on the walls around their homes and on the trees. There are scattered date palms decked out from tip to toe in colored lights. It's really a festive, joyous sight. There are two date palms that flank the entrance to the public park, and two others in the square. There's also the fountain—I nearly forgot that—in the center of the square, with lights of all colors around its rim, the ripple of the multicolored water, its gushing arcs, and other lights that hover in space as though they were moving with the clouds.

Here is her house. Madame Najwa's house. A spacious, two-story villa with light bulbs scattered over the entranceway lawn. You don't see the lights, or even the path traced by their rays. Translucent and soft, their glow surrounds the villa like moonlight.

He turned out the light in the room and lay down on the bed, the model twinkling atop the desk. Feeling pleased, he rested his head on his bent arm.

You hear about Madame Najwa but you don't see her. Then you do see her. You receive an invitation to her birthday party. She's never invited you before, a fact that used to pain you. You'd get wind of the legendary celebration, which was attended by the elite from both the township and the capital. Their luxury cars would nearly close off the street in front of the villa, and you would issue orders for an invisible guard to linger not far from the place. You also made certain that, by way of the guests' chauffeurs, she was apprised of the guard's presence.

For some of the guests who've come from the capital, a number of rooms have been reserved in a five-star hotel overlooking the river. You don't worry about them, though, since security around the hotel is tight and constant. You only want to know their names, and you're astounded to discover that they occupy no prominent posts, and that you've never even heard of them before. Madame Najwa has a number of guest rooms in her villa, as well as two five-bedroom flats in a large building. So, why the hotel? Perhaps it has to do with business being conducted in secret, and she doesn't want these people to mix with others beyond the hours taken up by the party, which allow for no more than formalities. Even so, you see nothing wrong with taking down their names in your private notebook, a habit you've acquired and rather like, as it's served you well on occasion.

The invitation card is pink, its message printed in gold ink, and there's a small flower made of white lace glued near one end. You shove the invitation aside, thinking about sending your regrets. You don't want to appear overly eager. You'd also like get back at her for ignoring you in years past. The time for the party arrives and you're still wavering, sitting behind you desk with your head bowed. Then you decide to go.

The navy blue civilian suit. You haven't worn it for a long time. You content yourself with a white rose wrapped in cellophane which you take in your hand. The villa garden is teeming with men and women in formal attire. You stroll through the crowd and no one takes any notice of you. You catch sight of Hafez Fawzi, and he waves to you, then takes you and introduces you to her. A forty-year-old woman with a comely appearance, she smiles at you, and you nod your head slightly in greeting. You're dazzled by the huge variety of foods and drinks, including roast sheep and turkeys hanging on spits over tiny hot embers so that they'll retain their heat, and a bountifully laden buffet displayed at a right angle in the corner of the garden and being serviced by butlers clad in white jackets.

The gathering is dotted with faces you've seen in the newspapers and on television, as well as those of senior government officials. You, the inspector of a regional police station, are gripped with fright. You stick close to Hajj Fawzi. Then suddenly you turn around and find that he's no longer at your side. He had been there talking and laughing with others. You take your leave before the party draws to a close, slipping out quietly lest anyone see you. You aren't angry, but of course, you aren't happy, either. The next day you receive an invitation to have tea with her in the late afternoon. This time, the invitation is by telephone. She chides you for leaving the party early, and you're pleased. You wiggle your feet with joy under the desk at the thought that she detected your early departure despite the fact that you snuck out!

You go to see her at the agreed-upon time. Without makeup and wearing a simple cotton print dress that reveals her arms and legs, she's seated under a parasol in the garden. You feel as though she's far more beautiful than she was on the night of the party. You speak freely with her about everything, even what you perceive to be problems at work, exaggerating slightly your uncompromising positions on things. She listens without comment. At the same time, though, she shows interest in what you're saying, nodding her head from time to time and smiling faintly. And sometimes she pats you affectionately on the hand. Never in your life has anyone, not even your wife, listened to you with such attentiveness. As she bids you farewell at the end of your session, she tells you that she's happy to have made the acquaintance of an open-minded man like you. She can't brook people with closed minds. They give her a headache.

You take leave of her in such a good mood, you dismiss the driver and come back on foot.

Along the way, you recall the things she said and reflect on them a bit. She knows that you're aware of the type of activity she's involved in, and she appreciated the fact that you didn't make even the slightest reference to it. Moreover, the great respect which you showed for her made her feel that you see nothing wrong with it.

She raises girls, or what you refer to as 'chicks.' You learn of the details later after relations between the two of you have developed and she tells you about them herself. However, your initial knowledge was limited to the general nature of her activity until that amusing incident. You're the one who described it as such, and when you related it to Madame Najwa, you were laughing.

"What a story!" she added.

Shaking your head somewhat ruefully, you said, "Really!"

The boy had come from a small, outlying village. Seventeen years old, he was wearing an old jacket over an old jilbab, and scruffy shoes without socks. The jacket had lost all its buttons and its neck hung open, revealing his dark-skinned chest. You know the type: boys who live their entire lives in small villages and who, when they have to go to the city, borrow a jacket and a pair of shoes from a student or whoever else. The few piasters he had with him, he had saved, not knowing what he might face. He'd come looking for his younger sister, who was thirteen years old. She was the only daughter among four sons, of whom he was the youngest. She'd been in the habit of accompanying him on donkey back whenever he went to the

96

fields, and she would get up on his shoulders in order to reach the high branches of mulberry trees. She hadn't been seen for three days, and of all his brothers, he was the only one who'd come out to look for her. All he knew was that she had come to Khaldiya. That's what he said when a report was drawn up at the station. He'd wandered all over the old quarter, then lingered in front of people's houses in the new quarter. All he could think of was that someone had played a trick on her and brought her to work as a maid in someone's house, and he was sure he'd meet up with her. He would either see her in front of a house, or she would look out of a window and, if he didn't see her, she might see him and call out to him. So he kept on roaming and, when it was late at night and his feet were worn out from all that walking, he headed for the police station in the hope that they'd received some news about her. He came up the stairs and looked around the empty lobby. The officer on duty gestured to him to come in. He hesitated and nearly turned around and left. However, he plucked up courage and went in.

One of the two women who worked for Madame Najwa in the area, but who didn't know her and had never even heard of her, had been found strangled in her home in the village from which the boy had come. The incident had been reported to the Khaldiya police station, and someone went there to investigate. Later, you began to speculate that the boy was the one who had murdered her. Perhaps he'd gotten wind of the fact that she had a hand in the disappearance of girls from his village, Kafr al-Shammam. Thirteen of them had disappeared so far, and not a single one of them had been found either dead or alive. The woman had worked as a seamstress, and from time to time, girls would gather at her house to sew jilbabs or just to watch. Sometimes she would ask the girls for help with the housework, or to buy things for her. The boy must have entered her house and started to choke her in order to force her to give him information. All she knew was that there was someone who would take the girls to Khaldiya. She had heard that. But she concealed from him the name of the woman to whom she had handed the girl over for fear of an investigation that would reveal her role in the operation. And perhaps there hadn't been enough time for her to tell him all she knew.

Since you had seen the thread winding its way toward Madame Najwa, you kept your suspicions to yourself. After all, if the accusation were pinned on the boy, much of what had been concealed would begin to surface. Not to mention the fact that your own negligence might be exposed. And even if you avoided that eventuality, you would lose Madame Najwa, whose acquaintance had come to be a source of refreshment to you, and about whom you'd begun entertaining certain pleasant notions. The justification you kept rehearsing to yourself was your pity for the boy, who had suffered greatly in his search for his sister. Besides, it was sufficient that he had lost her.

Later on, the seamstress's murder was pinned on an unknown individual, the motive being theft.

The officer on duty asked the boy, "And your sister's name?"

"Nawal."

"How did you find out that she'd come to Khaldiya?"

"I just did, that's all."

"What did you say, mama's boy?"

Wincing, the boy said, "I just found out."

"How?"

"People saw her."

"Which people?"

"At the railroad tracks. I don't know them."

"Do you have relatives or acquaintances here in Khaldiya?"

"No."

The officer on duty, who was also from a small village, had some fuul and falafel sandwiches on a plate in front of him, and the boy was trying to keep his eyes off the plate. Finally, though, the officer pushed the plate in his direction.

"Eat," he said.

The boy put up some resistance at first, then ate.

The officer said to him, "In a few days we'll know where she went."

After he'd eaten, the boy pointed behind the officer's chair.

"May I sleep there till morning?" he asked.

"It's not allowed."

Then the officer added, "It's only two or three hours till sunrise. Do you want to lie down in the jail cell?"

The boy agreed.

The officer on duty picked up the key hanging next to the desk, walked over to the confinement room and opened it. The boy went in, and he locked the door behind him.

Movement could be heard in the lightless room. Eyes that had been shut in slumber opened and gleamed in the dark. Legs that had been flexed stretched out to their full length. The boy ran his hands over the wall, searching with his foot for an empty spot on which to land. As he did so, a hand pulled him down into a sitting position. Then, within moments, a hand had been clapped over his mouth, while another hand lifted up the bottom of his jilbab. He struggled, but more than one hand paralyzed his movement, and he could feel hot breaths near his face. He saw someone coming from the other side and pulling down his trousers, his features indistinguishable in the darkness. He tried to break loose again, but the grips tightened around his body.

He started screaming bloody murder, beating the air with his hands, and they eventually let him go. And no sooner had the door been opened than he took off like a rocket. He pushed the officer on duty aside as he was about to come in, causing him to stumble and fall. On his way out of the building he took the steps three or four at a time. And that was the last that's been seen of him.

"No doubt he's home now in Kafr al-Shammam!"

Then you added with a chuckle, "After that, I don't think he'll be coming back again."

You chuckled again, and she chuckled with you. Then in some amazement she asked, "And the jail?"

"The jail. What goes on there is well-known. And there's nothing that can be done about it. So why should we take all the blame?"

"You said, 'Kafr al-Shammam.'"

"That's where the boy was from. Why do you ask?"

"Tell me: Is there a link between eating cantaloupe and girls' beauty?"

"What a question!" you exclaimed with a laugh.

She said, "The most beautiful girls I've ever seen are from there."

Then, detecting a quizzical look in your eyes, she continued, "That's right. I've seen a lot of them. And in more than one town. They're beautiful, that's for sure. But Kafr al-Shammam is another thing altogether. Incredible beauty. They'll drive you out of your mind: That rare wine color, the huge, honey-colored eyes and long lashes, the tall, willowy frame and the chestnut hair. And they're all like that. They only differ in minor details. Never mind the rough, chapped skin on their legs and arms, the 'thirst spots' on their faces, and the lice, of course. Those things can all be taken care of. And you ought to see them after I get through with them! They're something else. Sweet, fresh creatures that would be a delight to anybody. And you wouldn't believe that they're the same ones you'd seen wallowing in manure."

She suddenly stopped speaking.

"I thought you knew," she said.

"It's the first time I've heard about it."

"Have I made a mistake by telling you?"

"Outside my office, I'm like a lot of other people—quick to forget."

With her usual smile and warm gaze, she patted you on your knee and went on talking.

She has two women—the seamstress was one of them— who pick up girls from the outlying villages. They know the characteristics she wants in a girl. The girl disappears somehow and is sent to a house in a nearby village. In the early morning, a light carriage stands in front of the villa, carrying a lady and a girl as her servant.

"I have to get a final look at her myself. After all, it's a lot easier to send them back from the start than it is to send them back later on. However, it so happens that I've never sent a single one back. Even if I think she's just so-so, I say: Let her try her luck. And not one of them has let me down so far."

The carriage continues on its way to the train station, and from there they're taken to something like an army camp.

"You're the one who called it an army camp. Army camp, my foot!" She laughed and thumped you on your hand.

"It's a villa on the sea. A tourist village."

She owns four villas there, of which she uses two, while the other two are closed up until such time as she might need them.

"If you could see them after that!"

And you have. Once you were coming out of the villa when a taxi with a capital license plate pulled up. A dazzlingly beautiful, elegant girl got out, then bent down gracefully as she pulled out a small travel bag. She wore a short-sleeved dress that came down to her knees. You slowed your step as you approached the gate and looked at her. She'd nearly passed you by when you asked, "Are you Madame Najwa's daughter?"

"She's my aunt," came the reply.

Then she proceeded inside.

As you walked to the station that day, you cursed everything you'd ever heard or read about honor and virtue. It's all so much empty talk and nonsense. They never stop making big claims about how important they are, urging people to live by them. But for what? You yourself have seen these girls in the fields, on the backs of donkeys laden with bags of soil, along the drainage ditches, covered with mud from the riverbank.

They're no different from the animals around them. So, what's wrong with it? What's wrong with it?

The two of you got up from where you'd been sitting in the garden. It was time for her afternoon nap. As you walked unhurriedly toward the door of the villa, your hand grasped her bare arm as though you wanted to steer her away from a bit of mud you'd seen in her path. However, the touch of your fingers to the flesh of her arm said otherwise. She turned toward you with a smile.

"Don't be angry with me. I'm always honest with my friends. I have a 'gentleman friend' and I love him. I hope you'll understand and we'll go on being friends."

Your hand fell limply to your side and you returned her smile. You didn't really desire her in the way you'd pretended to. You simply thought this was what was expected of you, and you were keen to keep her friendship.

She contacted you one day and informed you that one of your colleagues had raided a flat of hers in the capital. She wasn't concerned about what they had taken from the flat. She was just worried about the three girls there and their guardian. They had taken them all with them. The flat, she said, was nothing but a small showroom for crocheted items. There was a sign on the flat's door and on the door of the building indicating this, and in the flat's living room there were glass display cases containing items for sale. She didn't want a shop that opened onto the main street for fear of having to pay taxes. And this had been her mistake. In any case, she asked you if there was anything you could do.

"I'll see," you told her.

You spoke at length with your colleague in the capital, who'd been a member of your graduating class, and in the end, he told you that the investigations appeared not to have been thorough. After all, there really were signs on the door of the building and on the door of the flat, and display cases in the flat's living room. You griped to each other about inaccurate investigations, which are sometimes biased. The people chosen to conduct them aren't competent or conscientious despite the critical nature of the cases involved, a fact that has landed both of you in outrageous predicaments. As the conversation drew to a close, he asked you to advise your lady friend to pay the taxes on her crochet sales and profits, since he was going to make reference in his report to the matter of tax evasion.

You're in your office, relaxing on the couch and contemplating the state of the world. You're also remembering the girl you met at the villa entrance, and the way she walked after she passed you, causing you to turn so that you could go on looking at her. She was wearing spike heels, and the walkways in the garden were covered with gravel. Hence, she tottered slightly as she walked, touching the gravel lightly the way a sparrow hops over the ground.

You gaze at her in your state of repose until she disappears inside the villa. You're about to doze off, when you remember something you heard somebody say recently. It pops into your mind just like that: "Opening the bottle costs dearly." When you first heard the phrase, it was followed by raucous laughter. You remember the place: Hajj Fawzi's villa, at a dinner party there. Who said it? Perhaps one of his friends. In attendance were a scrap metal dealer and the proprietor of the textiles factory in the old quarter, who'd cut a deal together for the sale of old machines in the factory. Hajj Fawzi said it, then it was repeated by the factory owner. They'd all been drinking a lot and were laughing at the drop of a hat. You, still being sober, wondered to yourself: How can that be? A Coca-Cola bottle doesn't cost more than half a pound. They all stopped drinking and carousing, their eyes glued to your face. Then all at once, they burst out laughing again for what seemed like a long time, with coughing, panting, and gasps, and you understood that they meant something else. As in most drinking sessions, the conversation revolved around women, and you finally got the point. You smiled and shook your head apologetically as they shouted merrily, "Yep, you've got it!"

Opening the bottle. It's a vulgar expression and you didn't like it. Even so, you found yourself smiling. After all, gatherings of this sort have unwritten rules that one is well advised to abide by.

You recall the expression from another occasion as well. Madame Najwa had learned of your decision to take a trip, and called you to inquire about your day of departure.

"Day after tomorrow," you told her.

She asked you if you would have any objections to traveling in her car rather than on the train, and you replied that you had none.

She told you that the girl staying with her would accompany you. She was sending her to a private hospital in the capital, and would be more assured of her safety and wellbeing if she was with you. She apologized for not being able to come along herself due to the back pains that she'd told you about before.

"Which girl?" you asked.

She replied, "You saw her when you were leaving my house one day."

"Ah, yes, I remember her now. I hope everything's all right?"

"She'll be having a simple type of plastic surgery on her nose. And if you wish, you can tell the driver when you'll be returning and he'll pass by your house and bring you back."

That marked the beginning of your use of her luxurious, air-conditioned cars.

The girl sat beside you in the back seat. There was a small refrigerator between the two front seats with chocolate and cans of juice in it. The girl smiled at you warmly, which confirmed to you that Madame Najwa had told her that you were a relative of hers.

She hastily devoured three chocolate bars, saying, "If my aunt saw me! She forbids me to eat things like this. She says they . . ."

As her voice trailed off, she looked out of the corner of her eye at the tubby driver, then looked down and smiled furtively.

"You won't tell my aunt that I ate chocolate?"

"No, I won't."

She leaned over and planted a kiss on your cheek. Meanwhile, she continued to make movements with her hands and feet that betrayed her humble origins. She did it without noticing it. The first time you became aware of it was when she brushed off some chocolate that had fallen on her chest. And when a small piece of it clung to her dress, she wet the edge of a handkerchief with her saliva and began wiping it off, then blew it dry.

Turning to you, she said, "It's gone now."

You asked if she was apprehensive about the operation.

Looking out the car window, she said without turning her head, "What operation? It's just a little pin prick."

Not understanding what she meant, you asked her, "Have you had this operation before?"

"This is the third one."

Then you finally caught on. It was something other than her nose she was talking about. Ah . . . opening the bottle. Bright-eyed and beautiful, she goes back to the way she was before. Madame Najwa had lied to you. However, you could excuse her for that, since it isn't proper to speak about such a thing, especially in mixed company. You looked thoughtfully at the girl. She rested the side of her head against the back of the seat, her eyes on the window and heavy with sleep.

You woke her up when you'd reached your destination. It was a clean hospital in a quiet neighborhood. The girl got out of the car with the driver, her small travel bag in hand. You followed her slowly. In the reception area she was approached by an official wearing a white overcoat, who smiled at her in welcome. Returning the smile, the girl stood on tiptoe and kissed him on the cheek. Then he took her by the arm and the two of them disappeared.

No sooner had you come down the steps on your way out than you saw him, leaning his back against the hospital wall. Gripped by a violent rage, you stormed up to him and said, "And here?"

As you lit into him with punches and kicks, he turned and clung to the wall, but the punches didn't let up for a second. He collapsed. The driver grabbed you and tried to pull you away, but you shook him off and proceeded to the car.

Pained by the sudden glare, he shielded his face with his arms. He was curled up at the end of the bed nearest the wall. He could hear his neighbor lady's voice: "We could hear your screaming all the way downstairs."

A number of hands reached out to pull his body straight and he surrendered to their attempts. His neighbor lady and others with her were standing in the center of the room. He always forgot to shut the door. The minute he felt drowsy, he would go to sleep. His pajama top was stained with drops of blood, as was the wall in the place where he'd been clinging to it. As soon as his nose rubbed up against anything, it would start bleeding, and it appeared to have bled a lot.

Eyeing him with concern, someone said to his neighbor lady, "Wash his face while I bring whatever I can find from my place."

His neighbor lady pulled him to the bathroom. He lowered his head over the sink and she rinsed his face for him. He asked her in a whisper to bring him another pair of pajamas from the wardrobe in the bedroom.

Another neighbor leaned over him and applied a solution to a wound over his eyebrow, followed by a piece of gauze and some tape. Looking into his nostrils, he asked him if he had these nightmares often.

"Sometimes," he said.

"It would be advisable for you to see a doctor."

"It's just a minor wound."

"I don't mean on account of the wound. On account of the nightmares. They've reached a point where . . . a neurologist . . ."

Then he turned to join the others, who were waiting outside the door. When he glimpsed the model and its tiny colored lights, he smiled in bemusement.

"Interesting," he said, then left.

Rising to his feet with great effort, he wet a piece of cloth with water and wiped the bloodstains off the wall.

Then he turned out the overhead light and the lights on the model and went back to bed.

Eight

He paced the room back and forth. He paused in front of the model and examined it for a moment, then resumed his pacing. Something wasn't to his liking. His brow furrowed and his hands behind his back, he stepped back from the model, then looked at it again. He hadn't intended for things to go this way, and when he'd been getting the model ready, he had wanted events that would lead to rewards and bonuses. But now, he couldn't picture the places and movement in the way he wanted to. Instead, he was taken unawares by people and places that had never even occurred to him. They imposed themselves, intruding on his plans, and everything began to move on its own. Events took place in steady succession, and he just followed them. He was seated on the edge of the bed, his head bowed and his hands between his legs. Perhaps he was blaming himself too much. After all, the major events were still in his hands, while the small things came and went, suddenly appearing, then disappearing. There was nothing wrong with that. On the contrary, it was only natural. However, small things could also have an impact. More than once, the course of events had been altered on account of them, and it had been more than two months since he'd drafted a single rewards report. Nor had he issued any decisions to impose penalties. After all, where were the events that might occasion them? He had distanced himself from them and gone running after other events that yielded nothing. Even so . . .

He pulled a chair out onto the roof and sat in a corner of the wall. Whenever he was in a bad mood, he would look out for a while from his elevated perch. The mood might not lift entirely, but at least he could think calmly.

He went back to the room and stood in front of the model. Maybe he ought to make some changes in it. The old quarter was quite sizeable. Of course, it was only natural that it should take up such a large area, since it contained the town's origins and roots, not to mention agricultural land and the factory. And here was the new quarter, which took up a smaller area.

What should the new quarter be like? It was redolent with perfume, remote, yet not remote. What change was called for? When he was engrossed in getting it ready, he'd been pleased, even excited. He'd been in a hurry to get to done it so that he could see the finished product. And then what happened? Events had taken themselves into their own hands. So be it, then. If rewards and punishments came of their own accord, fine. And if not, that was fine, too. No alterations were called for, and he wasn't going to change anything he had done. Maybe if he went out, he'd feel better. So he left.

He took a sweeping tour of the crowded streets. He walked along the river bank, then sat looking at the lights reflected in the water. He heard sparrows poking around in their nests on the branches of a tree that spread out above him.

"Tiny creatures," he mumbled.

Then he got up and went to the coffee shop.

Younis was in a distant, isolated corner smoking the water pipe. Unlike usual, he was depressed.

"I've never seen you smoke the water pipe before."

"I thought I'd try it."

"What's wrong?"

"My wife."

He fell silent. Then, looking downward slightly, he said, "She saw us."

"You and your neighbor?"

"Yeah."

Then he burst into tears, pressing his lips together. The sound of his muffled sobs continued to escape, despite his best efforts.

Wiping his eyes and his nose, he went on, "Yeah, she saw us. I turned my head while I was in bed, and I saw her standing in the bedroom door, leaning against the doorframe. I recognized the way she was standing, which indicated she was afraid she'd fall. We hadn't even locked the door. She didn't make a sound. Not a sound. I was naked and looked for something to cover myself with. She'd never seen me naked before. Whenever I take off my clothes at home, she turns and looks the other way. My neighbor was beside me. She lifted her head and looked at my wife. Then she got up, her top pulled all the way up to her bosom. She stood up on the bed and stepped over me. I had my eyes on her thighs, and when she arched her legs, they looked more and more beautiful. But my wife. . . . Only God knows, but I think my neighbor did that for my wife's benefit. She put on her robe and her slippers and smoothed her hair with her hands. She even put in her hairpins one by one, then walked to the door. My wife moved her body out of the way to keep her from touching her. My neighbor was acting like a crazy woman.

"Then she screeched at the top of her lungs, 'He's yours! Lick him!'

"Then she left.

"My wife was looking at me, doubled over. She hadn't been in good health in the first place. So there I was in the bed, not knowing what to do or say. Then she turned and left."

"What brought her to the flat?"

"What brought her?"

Holding back his sighs, he dried his nose and replied, "That's the way she is. And I'd forgotten. She never throws anything away. She bought some new kitchen utensils when we moved, and the old ones stayed in the flat. Who would ever have thought that she'd need any of them? But then again, why not? She's got a key, and back she came."

"When did it happen?"

"Five days ago. She said, 'I could forgive you for anything but this.' She doesn't eat a thing, and all she does is lie in bed. She wants to die. I come into the room, and she starts to cry and gasp, so I leave."

"And your children?"

"My children. . . . I don't know. They've got their sister. But if you'd only come with me!"

"Where?"

"To talk to her. She knows you. I've told her about you. She knows that you brought me extra work, and she used to call down blessings on you all the time. Just a word from you . . . "

"What do I say to her?"

"I don't know. It's enough for you just to come."

The two men left and went walking in silence. Distraught, Younis excused himself at the door to the flat and disappeared inside for a moment, then came back out. The flat was tidy and clean, its furniture still in good condition. There were pictures of trees, flowers and plants hanging on the wall. As they had on his previous visit, the children stood aside and looked at him from a distance. Then they came and greeted him. The girl had grown a bit, and was wearing pajamas with a silk robe over them. She smiled diffidently.

Then he followed Younis, who opened the bedroom door.

"Come in," he whispered.

The smell of incense always reminded him of death. Likewise, the dim light, the color white, the walls, the curtains, the bed, the bed sheet and blanket, and even her jilbab. Propped up with pillows behind her back, she looked at him as he approached her. Her hand was cold and frail, her face gaunt and pallid, and her eyes sunken with dark rings around them. Only her hair had retained its vitality. He sat on a chair that had been placed beside the bed for him, while Younis sat on the edge of a chair facing him on the other side.

"Thank you, Mr. Salem," she said, moistening her parched lips with the tip of her tongue.

Then silence reigned.

Younis looked aside, trying to hold back his tears, then got up and left.

A curtain billowed slightly, revealing the fact that one of the windows wasn't closed securely. His gaze settled on her pale, sallow fingers atop the blanket. Her little finger was arched, fiddling with a loose thread that protruded from the blanket.

She closed her eyes and her eyelids quivered faintly. She was content to die.

He waited for Younis to come back, then followed him out without a sound.

Nine

You see her again. The place is the same: in front of the station. She's wearing her long black jilbab, and the black veil on her head has slipped back, revealing some of her hair, one side of her neck, one of her ears and a gold earring that glistens as the light reflects off it. It's as if the scene is repeating itself, with the same open-toed shoes and painted toenails. This time, however, she raises a foot onto the first step. As you approach from the darkness, you don't take your eyes off her for a second. In fact, you don't even see the seven other people who've come with her, and who are sitting near a wall. She stops after ascending the first three steps, which pleases you, since you had wanted to be in a slightly elevated spot when you looked at her again. Your eyes meet, and she notices that you've taken a long look at her. Then your attention is distracted by a movement coming from the direction of the seven seated along the wall. As for her, her gaze is fixed and expressionless. And you had thought that given all the times you've thought about her and whispered to her in your imagination, she would surely have been attracted to you by now! You generally summon her presence before you go to sleep. You see her approaching you. You remove with your finger a lock that's fallen onto her face. Then you take her face in your hands and gaze into it passionately, caressing her voluptuous lips with yours. She rests her head on your chest. But the fantasy always stops there, and you go to sleep. Never once has it happened that you've disrobed her and embraced her. Something inside you warns you that it isn't time for that yet, and that if you tried to do so, she might disappear. From the place where you're standing on the stairs, you look at the seven, yet without seeing them. Then you look back at her. It's the same face you've known, even down to the tiny mole next to her ear that you've caressed so often with the tip of your tongue. Only now, it's tepid, distant. You turn toward the seven.

You ask them what they're doing here.

Unlike usual, your voice is devoid of anger.

Picking up on your conciliatory tone, the troublemakers don't rise when you speak to them. They don't even change the way they're sitting. His hand pointing limply inside the station, one of them says tersely, "There."

In other circumstances, he would have gotten a couple of resounding slaps. Rage almost gets the better of you. But you restrain yourself, staring at them motionlessly until you regain your composure.

Turning to her, you ask in a whisper, "And you?"

One of the seven replies, "Her husband, too."

You had wanted to hear her voice, the one thing that's been missing when you summon her presence. With fury sweeping over you, you descend a step wanting to show them a thing or two. Then you stop. As you come down the stairs, you come close to her. Very close. You take in the perfume of her body, her breath. Her posture hasn't altered in the least. Neither has her gaze. You can't bear her indifference. Suddenly you turn and hurriedly ascend the stairs. There's a rage in your step that you try to conceal. You return no salutes, nor even pay them any attention. You go inside your office and shut the door. You blame yourself mercilessly for the moments of weakness you just suffered. How could it be? How could you have allowed them? And her? Whatever the reason, you shake your head violently, refusing to recall the scene on the steps.

Some time passes and you calm down.

The station has received reports to the effect that the textile factory workers in the old quarter are preparing to strike. They've presented their demands in a memorandum that's been delivered to the factory owner, but he's rejected them. He wasn't even concerned enough to inform the station so that the necessary precautionary measures could be taken. In fact, you've shown no concern either. You've dealt with plenty of strikes during your career.

You tell the investigations assistant and the officers who've held a meeting, "The minute you've got them surrounded and you find them starting to flee—since the sight of the soldiers coming their way will make them panic—all you have to do is to set the force in motion in a provocative way: with shields, billy clubs, and helmets. The important thing is the steps they take. They have to be violent enough to shake things up. Then in a couple of days, you'll find them going back to their jobs."

"And if they don't go back?"

"In the whole time I've been on the job, they've always gone back. I'm speaking, of course, about the factories in other towns. Except on two occasions. On those two occasions, we brought in ten of them. You choose ten of the old-timers. When they get older, their demands increase: the expense of marrying off their sons, the cost of things that generally strike their fancy as they get up in years, and sometimes a second, younger, wife. You throw the ten in the clink, since they're always the motive force behind a strike. In a day or so, we always find them back at the factory. Then we let the ten go. In all their strikes, their demands are always the same: a salary increase, compensation, improved health services. But if you give in to them once, they win the game."

"Is there anything wrong with our taking precautions against violent clashes?"

"I have nothing against that. But take my word for it. They'll never seek out violent clashes. Workers who are asking for increased wages and health services don't get into fights. Beat them. Inflict some wounds on them. Keep them from going to work. Their strikes are never anything more than a kind of bubble. A way to prove their existence, or to go along with certain rabble-rousers. But they're not serious enough to be of real concern to us."

"How about vandalism on the sly? Burning down the factory, for example?"

"Look. Based on my experience on the job and in the world—and this is just between you and me . . ."

You chuckle, then continue, "Never once has it happened that workers have burned down a factory. Have you ever heard of peasant farmers burning crops or killing livestock just because they were angry? After all, this is their source of livelihood. No. You're mistaken if you think that I'm saying this as a compliment to them. Their strikes are in violation of the law, and we have no choice but to deal with them. However, what I want to stress is the importance of your having accurate background knowledge even if you say something that conflicts with it. This way, you're aware of the real situation no matter how you decide to conduct yourselves thereafter. This may also help you to decide where to stop."

Pleased by their looks of admiration, you proceed to your office. You said momentous things, and even you were startled to hear them rolling off your tongue. Of course, words are one thing, and action is another. You're not about to permit any strike no matter how unserious it is. Any departure from what is allowed is an insult to everything you stand for. And another thing you've kept to yourself is the turmoil that could be unleashed by the strike—a turmoil that could engulf the entire old quarter. The spark: that's your greatest concern. The one primary cautionary you received from headquarters when you first came here was: Beware of the old quarter. Let sleeping dogs lie. Don't let them take you in.

No sooner have you entered your office than you ask for reinforcements to be sent immediately from the Central Security Department.

"What's the matter?"

"A strike is looming."

"No problem."

The investigations assistant has brought in five factory workers and is trying to find out what's been going on in secret.

You've made your decision and that's that. You're going to deal with the situation as though a strike is going to take place—a strike with significance.

You come out of your office.

The five are standing in front of the lieutenant conducting the interrogation, and the investigations assistant is standing nearby, scrutinizing their faces as they speak. The lieutenant looks up toward you, and you signal him to halt the interrogation. You look into the faces of the five. Which of them is her husband? You try to guess. You don't even know his name, nor hers, for that matter. Which of them would best suit her?

All of them look wretched, and not one of them would you choose for her.

You send someone out to bring in one of the seven who are outside, and the woman, too.

You watch her as she approaches. Her steps are unhurried, her posture straight and unbending. And what did you expect?

You're looking your finest: standing erect with a baton under your arm, your cap cocked slightly to one side in the way that you know gives you a rakish air.

Observing her face out of the corner of your eye, you ask the man approaching, "Them?"

"Yes, them."

You turn toward her. "And your husband?"

Your question is met with the same impassive look, and from somewhere near you there comes a voice saying, "I'm her husband."

You shoot him a quick glance, which is sufficient to stamp his image in your mind. Having done that, you're anxious to get by yourself so that you can recall the image and reflect on it. You're baffled by her choice, and disappointed. You would have expected her to choose someone distinguished in some way or another. Of course, she may have had no say in the matter, as is the case with most marriages that take place in the old quarter. So she could be forgiven for that. However, her coming out after him to the station means that she's worried about him and concerned for his welfare. At the same time, it might simply be in conformity with custom and a matter of doing her duty, which is what you tend to believe.

You turn to the lieutenant.

"Close the case," you tell him.

Taken by surprise, the lieutenant looks up at you, then turns to the investigations assistant as though he's asking for his help, while the latter turns his face aside to conceal a grin.

You're in your glory, and a blaze inside you pumps the blood into your pallid face.

"This time," you announce, "we're going to release you."

Your glance travels from the six to her, then back to them.

"The next time, the treatment you get won't be so lenient."

One of the six says, "We still don't know why we're here."

You would have preferred that her husband be the one to speak. Preparing to leave, you say, "The next time, you'll know."

You cast a quick glance at her as you turn, searching for some response to what you just did. Her eyes, unchanged, reveal nothing. It doesn't bother you, though. You exit satisfied, knowing that the scene went just the way you'd wanted it to. And of course, she wouldn't let on in front of them.

There's no new news about the anticipated strike. Perhaps they're taking their time, or are just keeping things quiet. You don't trust the silence there. Soldiers from Central Security have arrived, and their vehicles are in two rows along either side of the main street that passes in front of the station. They're sitting lazily in the yard behind the station, peeling oranges with their daggers. Based on your orders, they form a double line and march along the riverbank with rapid steps, their shouts, "Ha! Ha!" piercing the atmosphere.

You smile when you hear them from your office.

Addressing one of the officers who are with you, you say, "Who knows? Perhaps they're all we'll need."

Reports come from the old quarter to the effect that school children will be demonstrating when the strike begins in solidarity with the workers' demands.

"From which schools?" you ask.

"The secondary schools."

"All of them?"

"All of them."

"And the girls, too!" you mutter.

That's what you'd expected. The flames are spreading, and the strike hasn't even begun yet.

It's easy to deal with workers: You put them under siege, issue some threats, and they disperse. Everybody goes his own way. But students are something else. It's difficult to put them under siege or to chase them down—on rooftops, in trees, and from street to street. And the rocks: You hear them whizzing by at the last moment, and you don't know where they came from. And the spears and arrows that they make out of tree branches. You have previous experience with them in other towns. And the colors they paint their faces with, like the Redskins and African tribal warriors. Even their war cries when they pass near you. They're all from the movies they see in the cinemas and on television.

In a meeting with your superiors some time ago you said, "If we can't close down the cinemas, then at least there's some choice concerning what films are shown there, and even more so on television. After all, what's wrong with musicals and variety shows?"

Then, in a fit of merriment, one of your superiors commented, "And instead of a troublemaking generation, we're faced with another type of generation that we haven't learned how to deal with yet!"

The station is on high alert. All vacations have been cancelled, and everyone is in field attire. Inquiries have been stepped up and the number of patrols increased. You ask the lieutenant who goes on the early evening patrol in the old quarter to let you take his place.

"What?" he shouts in disbelief.

"What's the matter with that?"

"You'd be targeted there."

"Where did you get that idea?"

"It isn't just my idea at all. But that's what we've gathered."

"So it's an inference you've drawn?"

"God forbid that they should do you harm. Word will get out that it's the inspector himself leading the patrol. As for me, I'm a mere lieutenant."

You take your patrol there. You take a tour around the factory, the schools, and the vital locations, then move down the streets. Based on your sense of things, there's nothing to suggest that they're preparing for anything. Even so, you pick up on a spirit of hostility. It isn't something that requires preparation. Rather, it comes all of a sudden. That's the way they are, as you've experienced in other towns. They sleep the night with nothing on their minds, and the next morning, things change.

You bring the patrol down the narrow street where her house is located. You recognize the house, which you've seen a number of times from a distance. The balconies facing the street are all open at this hour. The clip-clop of the horses' hooves usually draws people's attention. However, no one comes out on the balconies, as though it were a refusal to see you. You slow your pace as you approach her balcony, the horse nearly breaking into a dance step. There's a towel hanging on the clothesline, and next to it, a pink undershirt bordered along the bottom with lace of the same color. It doesn't move when the wind blows, and you think to yourself: It must still be wet. You pass the empty balcony, then continue on your way.

The next morning, you receive reports that the women and girls who work in the new quarter hadn't crossed the bridge that day.

"None of them?" you ask.

"Not a single one."

"A boycott," says the investigations assistant, adding with a smile, "then, the war!"

A lieutenant standing nearby states, "In the course of the investigations, one of them was asked about the reason for the boycott. All she said was, 'I've got no choice.'"

The investigations assistant says, "So, they're under orders."

You're irritated with the assistant, who's always in a hurry to comment on what's been said without thinking. And you're even more irritated by the way he wiggles his feet every time he speaks. Ever since he discovered your passion for the woman in the old quarter, he's been acting as though he has the right to special treatment from you. You don't allow such trivialities to interfere with what you do. However, sometimes he goes overboard with you, and you intend to keep him in his place.

You're bewildered by what the women and girls have done. Their source of livelihood, cordial relations with the households and commercial establishments where they work: Are they willing to throw all that away in a moment? And who will be willing to employ them after that?

You receive a call from Madame Najwa. She says no one has seen you for days.

You apologize, saying you've been busy and preoccupied of late.

In her smooth voice she says, "And when has that ever kept you from coming to see us?"

You've grown accustomed to her way of talking: a congenial preamble which you love and would like to prolong, after which she gets to the point.

She asks you, "What's your news?"

"Everything's just great."

"We've been hearing things."

"Don't believe everything you hear."

"And what do you advise?"

"I don't advise anything."

"My, my! A true inspector!"

"You know better than I do what's best for you."

"The best thing for me is for you to come over for tea."

"Another day."

"Fine. And what would you think of my going out of town for a couple of days?"

"If you absolutely have to, then all right, but on certain conditions. First, that you inform me of the day you leave. And you must inform me unconditionally."

"Of course I'll inform you. And second?"

"Second, don't let them be aware of your absence in the old quarter. You're forbidden to travel by train. Someone might see you. You must travel by car, and at night. There's a road out of here that leads straight to the superhighway, and from there to the capital. Don't let anyone see you. Do you hear me?"

"I hear you."

"No suitcases. Nothing that would attract attention. You need to act as though you were going out on a brief errand. Leave one or two servants in the house, and be sure the garden is lit up at night, with another light inside the villa. Have a safe trip."

You also receive calls from Hajj Fawzi and others. She appears to have informed them, and they want to confirm what they've heard. You tell them the same things you told her.

The new quarter looks like a ghost town. Many have left. The streets are nearly empty, and most of the commercial establishments are closed. Even the lights that used to be turned on in front of them at night have been left off.

You feel indignant as you check out the situation from the back of your horse. The exodus has expanded in a way you never would have imagined. They lack a sense of security. The silence

128

is heavy. There's nothing to suggest life as it used to be: no merriment or laughter in the streets. No honking of horns. No raucous celebrations ringing out into the stillness of the night. Nothing but the fountain, whose waters and colored lights still pour forth night and day, surrounded by empty seats.

You feel that their departure was a huge mistake, and that you could have done something to prevent or minimize it. However, you wanted to be the faithful friend and offer your counsel in an unobtrusive way.

As you conclude your tour, you catch sight of a stray dog standing hesitantly at a street corner. It sniffs the air, then continues on its way. The dogs in the new quarter are inside the walls. You study the dog for a while. You note the filthiness of its legs and the scruffy hair on its tail and back. It's just as you'd suspected. And your suspicion is confirmed when you see it lift its rear leg at the base of the wall around a certain villa, after which you see the urine running onto the pavement. Only a dog from the old quarter would do a thing like that.

So, if the dogs over in the old quarter have sensed the vacuum left by their leaving, how much more would you expect it to be felt by the old quarters' residents themselves! So far it's been limited to what you term "some crude jokes." A faint roar. And then what? Would their presence in the new quarter have prevented them from doing something if they'd wanted to? Even so, a sudden departure like this might tempt some of them to do something.

You step up your patrols in the new quarter and discontinue them in the old quarter. At the same time, you distribute a number of permanent observers along the length of the riverbank, where they're to hide behind the trees and watch out for any unusual movement in the old quarter. You believe you've taken the necessary precautions. The soldiers from central security are still available, lying around behind the station. What worries you is that you don't see anything unusual. Things are going along in their usual, familiar rhythm there. You see them taking their customary walks on the bridge after supper, standing with their backs against the railing, talking and laughing, then coming back again.

One day you were informed that a huge ruckus could be heard coming from that direction. At the same time, though, inquiries hadn't indicated that anything was in the offing. It was nighttime. You concealed yourself with your soldiers near the head of the bridge, while the soldiers from central security stood ready with their shields and clubs behind the trees in the park overlooking the river. The sounds grew louder on the other bank, while multicolored explosions could be seen in the dark sky. You looked on as the spray from the explosions dispersed and went out.

Then someone came and whispered to you, "It's a wedding, sir."

As if someone had just wakened you out of a heavy sleep, you shouted, "A wedding! What wedding?"

Retreating a step from the force of your shriek, he pointed distraughtly to the old quarter. "There. Somebody's getting married."

You stared into his face, trying to comprehend what he was saying. Then you became aware of the sound of the music, the rhythm of the tambourines and the ululations.

"Ah . . . a wedding."

Your body suddenly went limp, and you appeared lifeless atop your mount.

"A wedding," you mumbled again.

As you turned your horse around, the first thing you thought of was: Sleep till morning.

The next day you receive a call from Sa'di, owner of the textile factory. You don't take much of a liking to him, nor does he to you, and rarely have the two of you exchanged words.

He says, "They called me from the factory. There's a delegation coming. And I don't know whether to meet with them or not."

Despite his seeming unimaginativeness, he's cautious in the steps he takes. And he never lets on what he's really thinking.

"Give me a few minutes and I'll get back to you."

You need to think about what you're going to say to him. You're afraid he might use your words in a way that isn't to your liking. And how might he use them? You don't know. It's just a feeling you have, since you don't trust him. He could have dealt with factory problems in a way that didn't turn the place into a hot spot. And perhaps he has some motive for creating this tension, a motive that you're unable to discern. After all, people like him conceal what they want in the deep recesses of their souls.

A few minutes pass, then you tell him, "I'd advise you to meet with them in the usual way. Meet them the way you used to, and listen to what they have to say. Then make whatever decision you see fit."

"Is the situation that unstable?"

"What situation?"

You hear him laugh, then he hangs up.

Madame Najwa has told you things about him that make you loathe the man even more. He has an insatiable appetite for her girls. His requests are unreasonably frequent, to the point where she sometimes tells him that she doesn't have one available.

He flies into a rage, saying, "What do you mean? You've got an entire platoon, and you tell me that?"

Offended, she repeats what she said before.

"I have a carriage and driver," he says. "I can send them anywhere to bring her here."

"Have you ever in your life seen anything like it?" she asks me. The two of you chuckle, and she says, "And one day, he asked for two girls."

"'Who have you got with you?' I asked him. 'I always like to know who I'm sending the girls to.'

"'Nobody,' he replied.

"'And the two girls?'

"'They're both for me.'

"'For you?'

"So I flat out refused. I was mad, and I told him, 'My girls aren't the way you think they are. I don't teach them depravity.'"

"What depravity?"

"Depravity. Depravity."

She continues, saying, "After being with him, the girl comes back totally wiped out. She falls asleep, and after a while she's back on her feet. But the girls have started avoiding me and claiming to be sick when they know he's the person making the request. One of them said once, 'It's all bearable . . . except his bad breath!'"

You say with a smile, "I know what you mean."

Turning to you, she says, "You do, do you? Have you slept with him?"

You both laugh, then she leans toward you.

"By the way, I always forget to ask you: Why is it you've never requested my services?"

You smile at her.

"Don't you like my girls?"

"I do."

"Shall I pick one out for you? One that suits my own taste? A flat in the capital, or on the sea? Whatever you'd like. You can take a couple of days off, then come back to thank me."

Laughing, you say, "The only one I want is you."

"Very well, I'll finish my story for you: Ah, yes, Sa'di. I'm tired of him and his requests. In the end I brought him a girl . . . she, well, I never sent her to my friends. I was afraid she'd be too much for them, though you couldn't tell it from looking at her. And I said: If I don't hear from him soon, then at least he won't be asking for any more. And you'll never guess what happened after that!"

Pausing slightly before continuing her story, she takes her last sip of coffee and puts the cup aside. Then, noticing the ashes that have been falling from your cigarette onto the glass table top, she casts you a reproachful glance. Hastening to apologize, you take out a handkerchief to wipe them off. She stops you with a gesture of her hand and calls the maid, then gets back to her story.

"I waited for the girl to come back, but she didn't. A couple of days passed, then three, but there was no sign of her. So I called him. He said he wouldn't be sending her back, and that he wouldn't hear of her going to be with anyone else from then on.

"'Whatever you want from me, I'm at your service,' he said. I was bowled over. 'Fine,' I told him, 'I'll talk to the girl.' So I talked to her and she said she was happy. I found out from her that he brought her whatever she wanted: films, fruit, dresses, makeup, and that they were spending incredible evenings together. She said she was forbidden to go out, and that she couldn't go on visits or receive visitors. However, whenever when she was in the mood for an outing, he was at her beck and call. They'd take the car and disappear for days, then come back again. And she's still with him. It's been eight months now."

You receive reports of his meeting with the three-man delegation that came from the factory. They stood at the gate of the villa and asked the guard to inform him of their arrival.

The guard came back and said, "Wait. He'll call for you in a few minutes."

They waited an entire hour, after which a servant came out to inform them that he wouldn't be meeting with them after all. And back they went.

The investigations assistant was waiting for them at the head of the bridge. He brought them to the station and placed them in custody.

You come out of your office to check out the situation, and you see them in the jail cell. Her husband is among them. You don't take kindly to the disruptive way the investigations assistant comes up to you and says, "Have you heard about their meeting with Sa'di? He treated them the way they deserved. Leaders! Have you seen them? It looks as though they're the ones behind the strike. Read this."

They had with them the paper they were going to present to Sa'di. You look at it. The factory had been bearing the cost of workers' medical treatment, but three months earlier, the factory administration had decided that the costs would have to be borne by the workers and staff, and that they would be deducted in installments from their monthly wages. In the paper they had intended to present to Sa'di, they were asking him to intervene by issuing orders to the administration to go back to enforcing the previous policy, especially in light of the fact that most of the cases calling for treatment are work-related injuries.

The minute you finish reading the paper, the investigations assistant starts bellowing again: "They're up to the same old tricks! Blisters. Just a blister, and they're off to the doctor. Then they ask for all sorts of treatment. And the doctor writes a prescription even without a blister. The worker goes and asks for specific medicines for his children and relatives. Write, doctor, write! Sa'di is right to put a stop to this tomfoolery."

Appearing for interrogation, the three men stand in front of the same lieutenant. You're not far away.

The lieutenant says, "This time there aren't as many of you. There were five of you last time."

He scrutinizes their faces for a moment, then asks, "Which of you has been here before?"

Then, without waiting for a reply, he points to her husband: "You. And despite our warning. You're the one I'm going to address my questions to, and I don't want anyone but you to answer."

Addressing the other two momentarily he says, "Did you hear me?"

Question: "You've presented demands to Sa'di, the factory owner. What do you intend to do now that he has rejected them?"

Answer: "Nothing. It's his factory. What can we do but hear and obey?"

Question: "You said in a previous interrogation that you work in the factory's legal section. In other words, you've studied law. What do you think of the legitimacy of striking?"

Answer: "I don't know. We didn't study that at the university."

Question: "Based on sources other than your university studies, what's your personal view on the matter?"

Answer: "Striking in general is undesirable."

Question: "If this is your opinion, why did you take part in preparing for the factory strike?"

"What strike?"

It's the first time the strike has been mentioned since their interrogation began. The lieutenant erred in bringing it up. You don't want it to be known that you're aware of what's going on in the factory, since this will make them more circumspect, and cause them to do more to identify the individuals who leak information.

You've heard enough now. You know ahead of time the lieutenant's maneuvers, which will revolve around the strike in an attempt to pick up on any bit of information. Judging from their faces, they're more astute than the lieutenant thinks.

You go to your office.

You're in a reclining position when suddenly you sense that she's come. You sit up and stare at the closed door.

"She's there," you say to yourself.

Within moments you're standing in front of the small mirror straightening your clothes, grinning and muttering like an adolescent. Then you leave with your baton under your arm.

You find her standing in the same way she was on the two previous occasions. Her eyes are fixed on you and meet yours. You ignore her, turning your back to the door that leads outside. You speak to the lieutenant, who stands at full attention, asking him about the three detainees.

"We sent them back into detention, sir," he replies.

"Have you come up with anything?"

"Total denial. We're waiting for a decision from you, sir."

"And you? What do you think?"

"They have to be hiding something. They don't want to look like stoolpigeons."

"And then what?"

"Perhaps just the usual."

"The usual?"

"A little thrashing to loosen their tongues. Or a threat to the effect that the factory will be informed that they confessed. And just for emphasis, we can arrest some from the factory."

"Don't do either this or that. Wait."

You notice that your shoes are dirty. You forgot to clean them. You cast a fleeting glance in the direction of the outer door. She's still standing there as before, her eyes on you. Four other women accompany her, standing not far from her and looking stealthily inside. You return to your room and sit down behind the desk. You ring the bell and the orderly appears.

"There's a woman outside. Bring her here."

She comes and stands near the door the orderly closed behind him. You point to a chair in front of the desk. She comes forward and stands beside the chair. She looks at you, but you avoid her glance.

"Sit down," you say.

She remains standing. You want to appear cheerful, if even just a bit, but you don't know how. You want to speak with her about things that have nothing to do with the issue at hand, but you don't know what to say.

You ask her, "Do you know why I called for you?"

The look in her eyes reveals nothing. Your eyes are on hers. A moment or two passes and you nearly forget yourself. You lower your glance.

"Your husband is here."

You feel as though you're saying things other than what you want to. All you seek, all you're waiting for, is a sign from her. Just the slightest sign, and the course of the conversation would change.

Her hands are clasped in front of her abdomen. You note her long fingers and a costume jewelry ring with a stone set in it. Feeling your gaze perhaps, she drops her hands to her sides.

"I warned him last time. And if it weren't for your coming on that day, I wouldn't have released him."

Her face is expressionless, as are her eyes. Silence.

"This time, though, he's in a difficult position."

You rise and walk to the window. You look briefly out through the curtain, moving it with your finger. You look her way and find that she's turned to follow you with her eyes.

"How many years have you been married?"

She makes no reply.

"Whoever sees you would never guess you're married. Is he your relative?"

She makes no reply.

"What we know is that he doesn't spend his evenings at the coffee shops. He always spends them at home, and workers and staff from the factory come to spend them with him there. And they speak, of course, about things it isn't proper to speak about."

You come up and stand in front of her. Your hands are behind your back. You expected her to take a step back, but she remains where she is, returning your gaze.

"This time he's been dismissed from his job, and he might be imprisoned as well."

You fall silent, awaiting a reply. You wait for a long time, staring into her face. Your voice is gentle, but rasping as you say, "I can release him."

You fall silent again, yet without taking your eyes off her stony face. Your voice becomes more tender:

"And the other two as well. Right now."

You place your hand under her chin and experience the feel of her skin. Furrowing her brow slightly, she pulls her chin away from your hand.

"Say yes."

She furrows her brow even more, a fleeting glint of anger in her eyes. You look at her hesitantly. You want to say something but don't say it. You turn away from her and sit down at your desk with your head bowed. For a moment you sense her coming near you, but then you see her move away. You're not sure how much time passes as you sit there with your head bowed. You're distraught and blaming yourself. When she leaves, you don't hear her. You only notice that the door is ajar. You shouldn't have tried to bargain with her. In no time, she bolted and vanished.

You summon the lieutenant and order him to release the three.

"Give me more time, sir. We're just now getting started."

"You haven't got anything to pin on them."

"How about the paper?"

"What paper? It's an ordinary request that doesn't violate the law."

He stands there hesitantly for a moment. You know what he wants to say: "And when has that stopped us?"

He's used to harassing suspects until he's extracted whatever he wants from them.

As if to ease his burden, you say, "Give them some slack."

When you leave the station at a late hour, everyone is still in his office, and instead of one officer on duty, there are two, sitting side by side. The state of emergency is still in effect. And what would you do on a night like this anyway, when everyone you know has taken off for other parts? You walk toward the head of the bridge, where you're accustomed to casting a final glance at the old quarter. However, you don't reach the bridge. Instead, when you're halfway there, you turn around and go home. You take a bath and lie down in bed. You have no desire to blame yourself again.

Dim light from the living room steals in through the open bedroom door, mitigating the darkness there. You can feel drowsiness coming on. Lying on your side, you see her shadow in the bedroom entrance. From the time you came to know her, you've closed the front door without latching it or locking it with a key. After all, who but she would bother to come? You see her near the bed, her lips slightly parted.

She leans over you and whispers, "Have you been waiting for me?"

You gaze at her in silence, your eyes filled with longing. She whispers again, "Yes, you've been waiting for me."

She passes her finger over your lips, then stands up, pulls off her veil and tosses it on the chair next to the bed. She loosens her hair and it flows luxuriantly down over her shoulders. She unbuttons her black jilbab, then takes it off and places it with the veil. She's wearing a pink slip with thin shoulder straps. She reaches inside the slip and pulls on the bra that houses her voluptuous bosom. She pulls it off unhurriedly, then flings it on top of you. It occurs to you that this is a dream, which it is. Never has she removed her bra, nor has she felt such burning desire. Bending her knee on the edge of the bed, she whispers, "Are you angry with me?"

You prefer not to respond to her, you're so pleased that she's come. Then you begin to pant, your body stirs with longing, and you make room for her to join you. Your trembling hands pull off her slip and you envelop her body, plunging your face between her breasts. As she comes at you with a voracious passion, you hear a sound. It seems to be coming from far away. Then you hear it again. Out of the corner of your eye, you see him standing in the doorway, poking his head inside and looking around. It's him. Him. He approaches. He stands beside the bed and looks at the two of you. Disoriented and disheveled, you push her off you and fumble about with your feet in search of your slippers, but don't find them. Then you lunge at him, grab his neck and fling him to the floor. You kneel on top of him with your hands around his neck. He struggles beneath you, but you pin him between your thighs. Meanwhile, you keep up the pressure on his neck until at last you feel his body grow limp.

He lay in his bed, his mouth open and his eyes bulging out. His arm hung down motionlessly and the blanket lay on the floor. The lights on the model were out, and dawn was breaking over the horizon.

Glossary

arghoul a wind instrument consisting of two pipes of unequal length.

fuul Stewed fava beans, often put into pita bread and sold as sandwiches by street vendors. *Fuul mudammas* refers to cooked fava beans in oil.

gallabiya a floor-length collarless garment with long, broad sleeves and a wide, flowing skirt that allows for ease of movement.

jilbab a long, robe-like garment.

Shammam The name of the town in question, namely, shammam, means 'cantaloupe.'

Younis The English equivalent of Younis is Jonah, whom Muslims regard as a prophet.

Modern Arabic Literature
from the American University in Cairo Press

Ibrahim Abdel Meguid *Birds of Amber*
No One Sleeps in Alexandria • *The Other Place*
Yahya Taher Abdullah *The Mountain of Green Tea*
Leila Abouzeid *The Last Chapter*
Idris Ali *Dongola: A Novel of Nubia*
Ibrahim Aslan *The Heron* • *Nile Sparrows*
Alaa Al Aswany *The Yacoubian Building*
Hala El Badry *A Certain Woman*
Salwa Bakr *The Wiles of Men*
Hoda Barakat *Disciples of Passion* • *The Tiller of Waters*
Mourid Barghouti *I Saw Ramallah*
Mohamed El-Bisatie *Clamor of the Lake* • *Houses Behind the Trees*
A Last Glass of Tea • *Over the Bridge*
Fathy Ghanem *The Man Who Lost His Shadow*
Randa Ghazy *Dreaming of Palestine*
Gamal al-Ghitani *Zayni Barakat*
Tawfiq al-Hakim *The Prison of Life*
Yahya Hakki *The Lamp of Umm Hashim*
Bensalem Himmich *The Polymath* • *The Theocrat*
Taha Hussein *The Days* • *A Man of Letters* • *The Sufferers*
Sonallah Ibrahim *Cairo: From Edge to Edge* • *The Committee* • *Zaat*
Yusuf Idris *City of Love and Ashes*
Denys Johnson-Davies *Modern Arabic Literature: An Anthology*
Under the Naked Sky: Short Stories from the Arab World
Said al-Kafrawi *The Hill of Gypsies*
Sahar Khalifeh *The Inheritance*
Edwar al-Kharrat *Rama and the Dragon* • *Stones of Bobello*
Betool Khedairi *Absent*
Ibrahim al-Koni *Anubis*

Naguib Mahfouz *Adrift on the Nile* • *Akhenaten, Dweller in Truth*
Arabian Nights and Days • *Autumn Quail* • *The Beggar*
The Beginning and the End • *The Cairo Trilogy: Palace Walk,*
Palace of Desire, Sugar Street • *Children of the Alley*
The Day the Leader Was Killed • *The Dreams* • *Echoes of an Autobiography*
The Harafish • *The Journey of Ibn Fattouma* • *Khufu's Wisdom*
Midaq Alley • *Miramar* • *Naguib Mahfouz at Sidi Gaber*
Respected Sir • *Rhadopis of Nubia* • *The Search* • *The Seventh Heaven*
Thebes at War • *The Thief and the Dogs* • *The Time and the Place*
Wedding Song • *Voices from the Other World*
Mohamed Makhzangi *Memories of a Meltdown*
Alia Mamdouh *Naphtalene*
Selim Matar *The Woman of the Flask*
Ibrahim al-Mazini *Ten Again and Other Stories*
Ahlam Mosteghanemi *Chaos of the Senses* • *Memory in the Flesh*
Buthaina Al Nasiri *Final Night*
Haggag Hassan Oddoul *Nights of Musk*
Abd al-Hakim Qasim *Rites of Assent*
Somaya Ramadan *Leaves of Narcissus*
Lenin El-Ramly *In Plain Arabic*
Ghada Samman *The Night of the First Billion*
Rafik Schami *Damascus Nights*
Miral al-Tahawy *The Tent* • *Blue Aubergine*
Bahaa Taher *Love in Exile*
Fuad al-Takarli *The Long Way Back*
Latifa al-Zayyat *The Open Door*